CRASH LANDING

Frank settled back in the passenger seat of the solar-powered ultralite as it soared through the air. It was so peaceful up in the clouds, and quiet—almost too quiet, he told himself. He cocked his head and listened. He couldn't hear the propeller anymore.

"Trouble?" he asked the pilot.

"We lost power for a second," Theresa told him. She punched the starter switch once, twice, three times. Nothing happened.

Theresa smiled at Frank nervously. "Looks like we may be in for a rough landing. I can't get it—"

A sudden downdraft threw the plane into a dive. The nose pitched down violently, and Theresa's head was thrown forward to smash into the controls.

Frank was hurtling toward the ground in a flying coffin, with an unconscious pilot!

D0958588

Books in THE HARDY BOYS CASEFILES® Series

Available from ARCHWAY Paperbacks

THE HARDY BOYS CASEFILES NO. 50

POWER PLAY

FRANKLIN W. DIXON

AN ARCHWAY PAPERBACK
Published by POCKET BOOKS

New York   London   Toronto   Sydney   Tokyo   Singapore

AN ARCHWAY PAPERBACK *Original*

 An Archway Paperback published by
POCKET BOOKS, a division of Simon & Schuster
1230 Avenue of the Americas, New York, NY 10020

Copyright © 1991 by Simon & Schuster
Produced by Mega-Books of New York, Inc.

ISBN: 0-671-70047-2

First Archway Paperback printing April 1991

10 9 8 7 6 5 4 3 2 1

THE HARDY BOYS, AN ARCHWAY PAPERBACK and colophon are registered trademarks of Simon & Schuster.

THE HARDY BOYS CASEFILES is a trademark of Simon & Schuster.

Cover art by Brian Kotzky

Printed in the U.S.A.

IL 7+

Chapter

1

"THIS CHARACTER looks pretty suspicious to me," Joe Hardy said, studying the small photograph he was holding. "He's definitely up to no good." A young man with blue eyes and blond hair angrily glared back at Joe from the photograph. It was a picture of himself. "How come my photo ID looks like a mug shot of a convicted felon?"

His brother, Frank, clipped his picture ID badge onto his shirt pocket. His showed a young man with brown hair, intense brown eyes, and a reserved expression, as if he was waiting for something to happen. "If you'd try smiling instead of glowering at the camera," Frank suggested, "you might get better results."

Frank scanned the small, sparsely furnished

room they were waiting in. The clean office had no frills—just a desk, two chairs, and a metal filing cabinet. Frank, distracted by a soft click, turned his attention to the door as it was pushed open and two men walked in. One was the boys' father, Fenton Hardy. The other was John O'Hara, a tall, lean man with thick gray hair, a beard, and glasses. Frank and Joe had met him earlier that day.

O'Hara silently studied the two brothers before speaking to Fenton Hardy. "I know I've asked this already—but you are positive they're old enough to do this job?"

Joe bristled and stared over at the slightly shorter man from his full height of six feet.

"I'm old enough to vote," Frank responded before Joe could say anything. "And we're both old enough to drive. We've been helping our dad for a long time as private investigators, too."

"And we've got a perfect cover," Frank asserted. "Who'd suspect that a couple of high school students working here part-time were undercover detectives?"

"If your father wasn't busy," O'Hara told him, "I wouldn't even consider you and your brother. But since he's given me his assurances that he'll be able to supervise you, I guess I'm willing to give it a try."

"Good," Fenton Hardy replied, knowing that O'Hara had made up his mind before they came

2

into the room. "It's a pretty simple job. I've already filled Frank and Joe in on the basics."

"We know that Bright Futures Development has come up with a new kind of solar energy cell, and that you're worried about any leaks in your security to protect it," Frank said. "Obviously you can't have any of your competitors getting a look at the plans and stealing your ideas."

O'Hara nodded. "That's more or less it—but they're not my ideas, and it's not my company. In fact, the president and CEO wasn't exactly thrilled about hiring a private investigator."

Joe frowned. "Then what are we doing here?"

"Let's say I have a certain amount of influence," O'Hara answered.

"John's being modest," Fenton Hardy said. "He put up most of the capital for Bright Futures."

"You're the silent partner—the man with the money," Joe said to O'Hara. The older man nodded once. Joe's eyes moved around the room and then went back to O'Hara. "I see you spared no expense on your own office."

"I do my work out of an office in New York. I just use this room whenever I'm out here."

"Who exactly are we working for?" Frank asked.

O'Hara opened the door and gestured for the Hardys to move out into the hall. "You're working for me," he said as they walked down the hallway. "You're also working for Mike Barnes, the president of the company. He's an electrical engineer who worked for the government until he developed this new solar cell." He paused in front of a door that looked like all the others they had passed. "I think you'll find his office a little more impressive."

The door opened into a room that was even smaller than the one they had just left. A clean-cut man in his mid-twenties was sitting behind a desk at the far end of the room. He was wearing an expensive-looking gray suit, a white shirt, and a blue silk tie. Frank guessed that the guy spent most of his salary on clothes.

He glanced up at the Hardys with barely hidden disdain. "Ah, Mr. O'Hara," he said coolly, "Mr. Barnes is expecting you. You can go right in."

"Thank you, Tom," O'Hara replied. "Tom Kilman is Mr. Barnes's personal assistant," he told the Hardys. "He knows just about everything that goes on around here. So if you have any questions, just ask him. He'll be glad to help—won't you, Tom?"

Kilman smiled stiffly. "Of course," he said. "That's what I'm here for."

After they passed through the door to Mike Barnes's office, they found themselves in a tropical forest. Sunlight streamed in from a wall of glass that was angled like that of a greenhouse dome. Joe had to squint to see through the south-facing glass.

Almost hidden between two huge potted palms was a large oak desk. The leather chair behind the desk was empty.

"It's like a greenhouse in here," Joe remarked.

"That's right." He turned toward the voice from behind him. A short figure holding a watering can emerged from a cluster of potted plants. "A greenhouse is a classic example of passive solar energy, which is my business. I can't stress enough the importance of solar energy."

The man's curly brown hair was standing on end, and he looked as if he had missed his last two appointments with the barber. Baggy pants and a loose-fitting shirt didn't hide his round shape. He wasn't exactly fat, but he was close to it.

"Mike," John O'Hara began, "this is Fenton Hardy, and these are his sons, Frank and Joe."

The round man approached Fenton with an outstretched hand and a scowl on his face. "So you're the famous detective," he said as they shook hands. "I'm Mike Barnes."

"Glad to meet you," Fenton replied. "I don't know about the 'famous' part—but I know my business, and I usually get results."

Barnes moved over to his desk, pushed a pencil holder with blue pencils and a pile of papers off to one side, and perched on the edge. "I'm sure you do," he said, nodding his head slowly. "I'm sure you do."

5

"We can't afford a leak at this stage of our business, so we have to make sure our security is airtight," O'Hara added.

"What makes you think it isn't?" Frank asked.

"Nothing," Barnes replied, answering for the other man. "Nothing at all. In fact, I have a lot of faith in our security setup. I helped design it. You probably noticed some of our precautions on the way in."

Frank nodded. "Nobody gets in or out without an ID card or a guest pass. Video cameras in the halls are monitored from the security desk at the front entrance. Are there any other doors in or out of the building?"

"There are some emergency fire exits," Barnes answered, "but they're wired into the alarm system."

"So you have good protection against people who shouldn't be in here," Joe remarked. "But what about precautions against an inside job?"

"Only a few people have access to sensitive information," Barnes replied offhandedly. "I really think all these security precautions are unnecessary. We've never had a single incident—not even an indication that anyone will try to steal our new solar cell."

"I know," O'Hara said. "But I'm afraid I must insist on using these boys to help us."

"All right," Barnes reluctantly agreed. He shifted his gaze to the two brothers. "Your undercover jobs here will be to act as assistants to Alec Ward and Theresa Almonte. They're my best research and development people. Both crackerjack electrical engineers. Try not to get in their way.''

"They'll barely notice us," Frank assured him. "Do they know our real purpose in being here?''

Barnes sighed. "No, of course not. Ward's office is right down the hall. Room 113. I'd introduce you to them, but I have work to do." He jabbed a fat finger at the intercom on his desk. "Tom, take our new employees down to Alex Ward's office." He didn't wait for a reply.

"You two are on your own now," Fenton Hardy said. "See you at home tonight.''

"It's a date," Joe said, holding open the door for his father and O'Hara. He looked back at his brother. "Are you coming?''

"Just one more question, Mr. Barnes," Frank said, and held up a finger to indicate to Joe that he'd be right there.

Barnes raised his eyes. "Yes?''

"What's so 'super' about your solar cell?''

"What would you say," Barnes responded, "if I told you it could produce ten times more electricity than the best solar cell available?''

"I'd say you have something that a lot of people would like to get their hands on," Frank said. "If you aren't worried about someone trying to steal it, you should be.''

Frank and Joe followed Tom Kilman as he led

them down the hall to Room 113. Tom knocked lightly on the door. There was no answer. He tried again, harder this time, but still there was no answer. He jiggled the doorknob. It was unlocked. He pushed the door in and started back to his office.

"Hey, aren't you supposed to introduce us to Alex?" Frank asked.

"Mr. Barnes asked me to take you to Ward's office. I've done it. He said nothing about introducing you." Kilman sneered and turned to glide back down the hall to his office.

Frank peered inside and saw the profile of a gaunt figure hunched over a computer. The man appeared to be in his late twenties or early thirties. His stringy hair was long and tied back in a ponytail, but the top of his head was waging a losing battle against an aggressive bald spot. His wrinkled, untucked shirt, grubby jeans, and several days of beard stubble were in stark contrast to his spotless surroundings. Not even a poster or picture cluttered the walls. The single thing out of place was a compact disk on top of the computer screen.

The man at the computer didn't act as if he noticed Frank and Joe standing in the open door. He seemed to be completely absorbed in another world—either the one on the computer screen or the one coming through the headphones attached to the CD player clipped on his belt.

Frank walked up to him and waved a hand in his face.

The man jumped and turned his head to glare up at Frank. "What do you want?" he asked in an irritated voice, pulling off his headphones. Frank could hear the faint rumblings of classical music, which would have to have been deafeningly loud through the headphones. "Can't you see I'm busy?"

"Sorry," Frank replied. "We're looking for Alec Ward. We're his new assistants."

The skinny figure eyed Frank suspiciously. "I'm Ward, but I didn't ask for any assistants. I really don't have time for this or you."

He put the headphones back on and continued staring at the computer screen.

"So that's Alec Ward," Joe remarked. "Not exactly the original fun guy, is he?"

"He's not paid to have fun," a woman replied. "He's paid to think, and he does that very well."

Frank and Joe spun around to face a tall woman with bright red hair and freckles set against pale white skin.

She chuckled softly. "I guess nobody told you about Alec. He's not the social type. I'm Theresa Almonte. What's this about Alec's getting assistants?"

"Not just Alec. We're your assistants, too," Joe added.

Frank shrugged. "We just go where they tell

us to go. I'm Frank Hardy, and this is my brother Joe.''

"I don't know where we'll put you," she said, gesturing around the small space. "My office isn't any bigger than this—and it's a lot messier. But I'm sure we can find some place for you. Don't think I don't appreciate having you, I just wish we'd been told we're getting assistants." She glanced at her watch. "It's almost five now. Why don't we meet here first thing tomorrow morning?"

"How about first thing after our classes tomorrow?" Joe countered. "Two's the earliest we can get here. We're only part-time."

"That's even better," she said. "I'll be busy most of the morning anyway—and I don't think you're ready for several hours alone in a small room with Alec."

When the Hardys got to the Bright Futures office at two o'clock the next afternoon, they found Theresa Almonte alone in Ward's office.

"Ah, there you are," she said, greeting them. "Ready for your first assignment?"

"Where's the music lover?" Frank asked.

"*That's* your first assignment," she replied. "Alec should have been here hours ago. He hasn't called in, and I can't get an answer at his house on the phone. He can't hear anything over those headphones he's plugged into all the time.

Anyway," she continued, "I really need to talk to him."

"And you want us to find him," Frank said.

Almonte nodded. "If you wouldn't mind." She handed Frank a piece of paper with his address. "Just tell him to call the office."

"Well," Joe muttered as they walked back down the hallway. "This is one way to get the job done. We can test the security system by going in and out of the building all day long."

Frank drove their black van to the address on the sheet of paper. It was a three-story, brick apartment building. Under each mailbox was a buzzer, and Ward's name was on the box marked 3E. Frank pressed the buzzer, not really expecting an answer—and there wasn't any. The front door was open, so they walked up to the third floor and found apartment 3E.

Frank rapped loudly on the door. "Mr. Ward?" he shouted. "Are you in there?" Again, he wasn't really expecting an answer. He also wasn't expecting the door to swing open when he pounded on it. And he wasn't expecting to see Alec Ward sprawled out on the floor, head-phones clamped over his ears.

"I don't suppose he's just taking a little nap," Joe whispered.

Frank shook his head and pointed to a dark stain on the carpet around Ward's head. "I don't think so," he said grimly.

Chapter

2

FRANK KNELT DOWN and touched Ward's arm. It was cold. Then he checked the dark stain on the rug and found it was dry. "Looks like he's been dead a few hours," he said as he stood up.

Joe's eyes darted around the room. It was neat and orderly, just like Ward's office. An expensive stereo system and a huge collection of compact disks covered most of one wall. "No signs of a struggle," he observed.

"No sign of the murder weapon, either," Frank pointed out. He pulled a handkerchief out of his pocket and walked over to the telephone. He draped the cloth over it and lifted the receiver.

"Do you think somebody whacked him with the phone?" Joe asked doubtfully.

"No," Frank answered. "We have to call the police—and I don't want to mess up any fingerprints." He picked up a blue pencil on the telephone table and used it to dial 911.

In a few minutes the building was surrounded by strobing blue lights, and the apartment was packed with blue uniforms. One officer was marking the outline of Ward's body on the carpet while another one scraped samples of the purplish rug stain into a plastic bag. Frank and Joe were in the bedroom giving their statement to Officer Con Riley when Chief Collig strode in. The boys followed Riley out to greet the chief.

Collig shot an angry glance at the Hardys. "What are *they* doing here?" he demanded sharply.

Joe was about to say something when Con Riley stepped forward. "They found the body, Chief. Frank called it in."

Good old Con, Joe thought. Every detective should have at least one friend on the local police force. But he knew that most cops took a dim view of private operatives, and Chief Collig was a classic example.

"I suppose they were just out for a stroll," the police chief said sourly, "and they happened to wander in here and stumble over the body."

"Something like that," Joe quipped. "Just add the fact that we're working for the same company and we were sent over here to get him, and then you pretty much have the whole picture.''

Collig looked at the body on the floor. "What company would that be? Murder, Inc.?"

"Bright Futures Development," Frank told him. "It's a solar energy company."

"Better get the head of the company over here," Collig said to one of the officers. "Maybe he can shed a little light on this."

"I've already called him," Riley said. "He should be here any minute."

"Any relatives? A girlfriend?" Collig asked.

"None so far—it seems he was a real loner. Maybe a bit eccentric," Con said.

The police chief lost interest in the Hardys and Con, and went over to examine the body. "What was the time of death?" he asked the medical examiner.

"My preliminary estimate is between eleven-fifteen and eleven forty-five last night," the doctor said, stripping off his rubber gloves.

Frank nudged his brother and nodded toward the door where Mike Barnes was standing. He seemed reluctant to enter, and none of the police had noticed him yet.

Frank moved over to his boss, and his brother quietly followed.

"This is horrible," Barnes said, shaking his head. "Just horrible. I'm sorry you had to find him. Who would do something like this?" The words tumbled out of him in rapid and disjointed succession.

"We were hoping you'd have some idea who it might be," Frank replied. "John O'Hara was worried about industrial espionage—but what about sabotage?"

Barnes stared at Frank. "You think somebody killed Alec to hold up production of the super solar cell?"

"You said he was your most important research and development person," Frank said. "What was he working on specifically?"

"He was building a better prototype of the cell," Barnes answered.

"In a tiny room, with only a computer?" Joe asked.

"All the refinements are done by computer first. It's a lot cheaper to use it than to keep building cell after cell," Barnes said.

"Maybe somebody doesn't want *anybody* to have that cell."

"Or at least doesn't want anybody else to have it if they can't have it themselves," Joe added.

"It's possible," Barnes admitted.

"What about your competition—other solar energy companies?" Frank suggested.

"There are lots of companies working with solar power," Barnes said. "But our biggest competitor is Solex, over in Lewiston."

"That's the company that's about a half-hour drive from here?" Joe asked.

Barnes nodded. "It's run by a man named Ben Watson."

"Do you know him?" Frank asked.

"We've met," Barnes said vaguely.

A large hand landed heavily on Frank's shoulder

"Who's your friend, Frank?" Collig asked.

"Chief Collig, this is Mike Barnes, the president of Bright Futures—the company that Alec worked for," Frank replied.

"Thanks, boys, I don't think we'll be needing you anymore today. I'm sure you can find something else to do while we get on with our investigation," he added.

"I'm sure we can, too," Frank replied. "As a matter of fact, we were just on our way out to do it."

"You know," Joe said, staring through the windshield of the black van, "I don't think Chief Collig likes us very much."

Frank looked up from the street map he had opened across his lap. "He's just trying to do his job. He doesn't want us to—" He glanced at the map. "Turn left here."

"He doesn't want us to turn left here?"

"No—I mean, yes—I mean *turn left here!*"

"No problem," Joe said, and flipped on the

turn signal before pulling the wheel to the left. "Why didn't you just say so in the first place?"

Frank shook his head and sighed. "I don't know how I ever solved a single case, working with you."

"*You* didn't," Joe replied. "I'm the brains behind this outfit. Every once in a while I just let you *think* you solve a case."

"Well, stuff your brains back in your head and turn this crate around," Frank said. He turned his head to catch a passing sign on the right. "You just missed the place we're looking for."

Joe slowed down, checked the sideview mirror, and swung the van around in a quick U-turn. This time he saw the sign. "Solex, Inc.," he read aloud. "Sounds like some kind of household cleaner. They should come up with a better name, don't you think?" He pulled the van into the visitors' parking area.

"I'm sure Mr. Watson will be eager to hear your marketing suggestions," Frank said, climbing out of the van and heading for the front entrance.

"How are we going to get him to talk to us at all?" Joe asked when they were in the lobby.

"Don't worry," Frank answered in a hushed voice. "I have a plan."

Joe groaned softly. "I *hate* your plans. Why do they all have a part that says 'Joe does something stupid or dangerous here.' "

Frank took his brother's arm and guided him

toward the receptionist. "Don't worry. This time you don't have to *do* anything. You just have to *look* stupid."

"Oh, what a relief," Joe muttered.

"Excuse me, miss," Frank said to the blond, perfectly groomed receptionist.

She barely glanced at him before turning her attention back to the computer terminal on her desk. "If you're here about the part-time job," she said in a British accent, holding out a sheet of paper, "you'll have to fill out an application."

"Excuse me?" Frank responded.

"And there's a typing test, too," she added, as if she hadn't heard him.

"There must be some mistake," Frank said. "We're here to see Mr. Watson."

"Do you have an appointment?" she asked in an officially polite tone, still staring at the computer instead of Frank.

Frank nodded. "Yes. I'm Frank Hardy, and this is my brother, Joe."

She tapped a few keys and studied a display on the monitor. "I'm sorry, sir. I don't see your name here."

"Well," Frank said, "our lawyer told us Mr. Watson's lawyer informed him that Mr. Watson agreed to meet with us today."

She focused all her attention on him now. "Your lawyer?" she responded in a puzzled tone.

Frank nodded. "Yes. You see, my brother was blinded by one of your solar barbecues. We

18

were told that Mr. Watson wanted to avoid an unpleasant public trial, and—"

"Let me just ring his office," she interrupted in a nervous tone.

"That would be very kind," Frank replied. "Close your mouth, Joe," he whispered to his brother. "You look like an idiot with it flapping in the breeze."

A few minutes later Joe was seated across a desk from a man with a broad nose and a strong, square chin. His jet black hair was brushed straight back and neatly trimmed.

"Thank you for fitting us into your busy schedule, Mr. Watson," Frank said from the seat next to Joe.

The man behind the desk studied Joe intently for a moment. "What's all this about? You certainly don't appear to be blind, and we don't make a solar barbecue. You've got exactly thirty seconds to give me a reason why I shouldn't have you both thrown out of here right now."

"Alec Ward," Frank said.

Watson's eyes narrowed. "What about him?"

"So you know him," Frank responded.

"I know who he is," Watson said. "He works for Mike Barnes. I heard he was hired to work out the production problems for Mike's new solar cell. Is Ward in some kind of trouble?"

"You could say that," Joe spoke up. "He's dead."

"I'm sorry," Watson said in a neutral voice. "But what does that have to do with me?"

"He was murdered," Joe answered. "Where were you around eleven-thirty last night?"

Watson glowered at him. "What is this? Some kind of shakedown? Well, it won't work. I was here in my office until almost one in the morning. In fact, I think I got a couple of phone calls around eleven-thirty."

"Can anybody verify that?" Frank asked.

'Sure," Watson snapped. "The people who called me, and the police can check the phone company records. I don't know who you guys are"—he grabbed a phone and rapidly punched some buttons—"but you're history now."

Frank and Joe left the building one step ahead of the security guards Watson had called to throw them out. It was early evening when they got back to Bayport. At the Bright Futures office they learned that Theresa Almonte had gone home. Mike Barnes wasn't there, either, but he had left a message for the Hardys.

"Did he fire us?" Joe asked as his brother read the note.

"No," Frank said. "He wants us to meet him at his house at eight-thirty."

Joe checked a clock on the wall. "Great. That gives us enough time to swing by the house and grab some dinner first."

* * *

After filling their father in on the day's activities and filling their stomachs, the boys drove to Barnes's secluded house on the outskirts of Bayport.

There was no light on, and in the darkness the structure looked like an indistinct lump to Joe. As they walked up to it, he could see that the lump was a hill, and the house was built into the side of it.

A pair of headlights appeared in the driveway just then. The car that pulled in was the quietest and strangest Joe had ever seen. It was built low to the ground like a race car, but it was almost as wide as a truck. The surface was some kind of dull black material.

Mike Barnes got out of the car and ran into the garage to turn on an outside light. "What do you think of it?" he asked, gesturing at the vehicle. "It runs on nothing but pure sunshine."

Joe could get a good look now. The car wasn't painted black—it was completely covered with solar cells. Joe was impressed, but confused. "How can you drive a solar car at night?"

Barnes laughed. "Solar energy wouldn't be much good if you could use it only in the daytime. Luckily, somebody had already invented batteries—so I didn't have to do that. The solar energy that the cells collect during the day is pumped to a series of storage batteries under the front seat."

"Do you just leave it out here in the open at night?" Frank asked.

Barnes nodded back at the garage. "I keep it in there. There's a skylight in the roof so it can charge up on the early morning rays.

"I hope you don't mind coming all the way out here," he said as they went into the house. "After what happened today, I wanted to have a talk."

Frank nodded, encouraging him to continue.

"I got a call from Ben Watson early this evening," Barnes said. "He wasn't very happy about your visit."

"Does he know we're working for you?" Joe asked.

"I don't think so," Barnes replied. "He asked, but I dodged the question. Did you find out anything?"

Frank shrugged. "Not really. What about the police? Anything new while you were with Collig?"

"Alec was killed by a blow to the head," Barnes said.

"No big surprise there," Joe said. "There was a wound on the head and a pool of blood around it. What about suspects?"

Barnes shook his head. "They don't have much to go on, and nobody has jumped in to confess. They talked to Theresa while I was there, but I guess she wasn't much help. They did ask her where she was last night. . . ." His voice trailed off, and he suddenly seemed to be uncomfortable.

"And?" Frank prodded.

Barnes sighed and then continued. "This is a little difficult. She said she was home alone, but she can't prove it."

"That hardly makes her a murder suspect," Frank said.

"Well, that's not all," Barnes replied. "Theresa came to see me a few days ago, claiming that Alec had stolen some of her work and was taking credit for it. She said if I didn't do something about it, she would put an end to it!"

Chapter

3

"Did you do anything?" Joe asked.

Barnes looked at the ground and shook his head. "I was busy and hoped it would all blow over after a while."

"It looks like it blew up instead," Joe remarked.

Frank filed this new information with what they already knew. According to his math, none of this added up to murder yet. "I imagine the police wanted to know where you were last night, too," he said to Barnes.

"Yes," Barnes said. "If I had been home, I would probably have had trouble proving it, too, since I live alone. Luckily, I was in my office."

"Was anybody with you?" Joe asked.

Barnes shook his head. "No, but you can't leave the building after six without signing out at the security desk at the front door. I signed out a little after midnight. The guard on duty can verify it."

"If Almonte did it," Frank said, "the police are going to need a lot to make a case against her. We're in the perfect position to keep a close eye on her."

"Right," Joe said. "She thinks we're just a couple of part-time research and development assistants."

"I don't know," Barnes responded uneasily. "This case is a lot more than a routine check of our security measures now."

"Yes, it is," Frank agreed. "One of your key employees is dead, and another one may be a suspect in that murder. Until you know if Theresa Almonte is guilty or innocent, you need us more than ever."

"All right," Barnes said without much enthusiasm. "But if I think you're in any danger, I'm pulling the plug, and you're out."

The sun was still high when Frank and Joe drove into the Bright Futures parking lot the next afternoon. After Joe climbed out of the van, he stretched his arms and tilted his head back to soak up some of the warm spring rays. "Look, Frank," he said with a grin, "I'm a solar collector."

Frank hadn't heard him because someone else had caught his eye. "Ms. Almonte!" he shouted.

25

"Wait up!" He jogged across the blacktop to her. Joe caught up a few seconds later.

Theresa Almonte had stopped with her car door half open to look back over her shoulder. "I didn't expect to see you two again," she said. "You had a pretty rough first day." She smiled weakly.

"Let's just say it wasn't exactly what we expected," Frank replied. "But it's a job. If you're taking off early, we can go clean your office or something."

"I wish I could take the day off," she said with a sigh. "But without Alec, I've got twice as much to do. I'm on the way out to the farm to check on some tests."

"The farm?" Joe responded.

She gave him a curious look. "Nobody told you about the farm? Well, everybody should see the farm at least once—and there's no time like the present. Hop in, and I'll take you out there."

Joe cast an envious but doubtful eye on the red two-seater sports car. "It'll be a little cramped, don't you think?"

"Why don't we just follow you in our van?" Frank suggested.

"Good idea," Almonte said. She glanced at her watch. "We'd better get going because I have to make the most of the daylight."

The Hardys hopped back into the van and pulled in behind the red sports car as it headed out of the parking lot. A twenty-minute drive

26

took them past the Bayport city limits to the open countryside. Cows and horses roamed in green pastures, and Frank had to veer the van around more than one tractor plodding down the two-lane highway.

Almonte's car slowed beside a long, high chain-link fence. Through the steel mesh, Joe and Frank could see rows and rows of flat, rectangular panels gleaming in the sunlight. Each panel was about fifteen feet long and five feet wide, and they were all tilted up at the same angle.

The sports car continued on and stopped at a gate, where Almonte exchanged a few words with a uniformed guard.

"If this is a farm," Joe said to his brother, "I don't think we'll be milking any cows."

Frank smiled as the guard waved them through the gate. "It's a solar farm, Joe. Those panels are lined with solar cells, turning sunlight into electricity. It's like any electric plant, but it uses the sun rather than coal or water power to produce electricity."

Almonte parked her car in front of a wide, windowless one-story building. After Frank pulled up beside the sports car, the two brothers got out and took in their surroundings. There were two other buildings, both smaller. None of them seemed like much more than large sheds, although Frank noticed that one of them had a large picture window that looked out on the field of solar collectors.

Theresa Almonte walked over to them. "Not the kind of farm you were expecting, I take it."

"We decided you weren't milking cows out here," Frank replied, stealing his brother's line. "But what are those things on the other side of the solar panels?" He pointed to a cluster of bowl-shaped objects that looked like satellite dish antennas.

"Those are solar energy collectors, too," she told them. "Those dishes are lined with highly polished mirrors, all focused on a central core of photovoltaic cells."

Joe frowned. "Rewind that for me. I got everything but the last part about the photo gizmos."

"Photovoltaics," Frank said slowly. "Light hitting the photovoltaic element frees electrons in a silicon semiconductor, creating a low electric current."

Almonte looked at Frank. "Not bad. Where'd you learn all that?"

Frank shrugged casually. "I read a lot."

"Well, here's something you won't find in your books," Almonte said. "We're not using silicon, and the current isn't exactly low."

"What *are* you using?" Joe asked. "And how low *isn't* the current?"

"It's a secret," she whispered loudly. Then she turned away and headed for the largest of the three buildings. "Come on," she called over her shoulder. "I want to show you something."

After she unlocked the main door, the Hardys

followed her inside. "What's in he—" Joe started to say before she flipped on the lights. Then he could see that the entire building was one huge room, like a warehouse, or—

"An airplane hangar," Frank uttered with a mixture of surprise and delight. Flying was up at the top of his list of things to do whenever possible. Even though he was only eighteen, he recently had gotten his pilot's license.

The plane in front of him was unlike any he had ever seen before. It was about the same size as the single-engine prop jobs he was certified to fly, but the similarity ended there.

The first thing he noticed was the propeller. It was behind the fuselage instead of in front of it. The wingspan was much wider than on the planes Frank had handled, and there was also a short, stubby winglike structure just beneath the nose.

Frank walked around the plane slowly. The streamlined cockpit had two seats, one behind the other. Up close, he could see that the surface of the large wings was covered with solar cells.

Almonte patted the side of the plane. "This is the real reason I came out here today. After I saw Mike's solar car, I convinced him to let me build a plane. The electric engine is powered entirely by super solar cells."

She glanced at Frank and smiled. "I see you've got the bug, too."

29

Frank stopped staring at the plane. "What bug?"

"The flying bug," she answered. "There's nothing quite like it, is there?" She didn't wait for a response. "Let's open the hangar doors and get this baby out in the sun where she belongs."

Frank and Joe each took hold of one of the heavy hangar doors and hauled it back on its sliding tracks. Then the three of them pushed the plane outside.

As he was shoving, Joe realized he could have moved the plane all by himself. "It doesn't weigh a whole lot," he commented.

"No, it doesn't," Almonte said. "It's really not much more than a glorified ultralite. It takes the most power to get a plane off the ground, and even with our improved solar cells, this is about the heaviest load we can lift."

"Can it really handle two people?" Frank asked hopefully. "Or is the seat behind the pilot just for show?"

Almonte lifted the clear glass canopy, reached in, and pulled out two helmets. "We had to make it fly with two people. There was no way Barnes was going to let me build it if he couldn't ride in it, and he doesn't have a pilot's license."

"I do," Frank said.

Almonte tossed him one of the helmets. "So do I, but you can come along for the ride, if you want."

Frank glanced down at the helmet in his hands and then over at his brother.

"Go on," Joe said. "I'll find something to do—maybe slap on some heavy-duty sun block and lie around not getting tan."

Frank's eyes shifted back to the solar plane. Almonte was already in the pilot's seat. She hit the ignition switch, and the rear propeller started to spin, faster and faster, until it was just a blur. "Let's go!" she called out. "I don't want to waste a lot of juice on the ground!"

Frank gazed up at the wide open blue sky. Then he slapped the helmet on his head and climbed into the seat behind Almonte. He tapped the helmet with his knuckles. "Is this really necessary?"

"Yes," she responded firmly. "And so is the shoulder harness. This is an experimental aircraft. We don't take any unnecessary risks." She reached up, pulled down the canopy, and secured it with two latches, one on each side of the cockpit. Then she gripped the controls, and the plane started to move.

Except for Almonte's helmet in front and the tail of the plane in the rear, Frank had a clear view on all sides through the molded glass bubble. He looked out at the "runway," which wasn't much more than a slab of concrete. Frank had seen longer driveways. They started to pick up a little speed as they rolled along—but the end of the concrete was coming uncomfortably close. Frank braced himself for an unplanned stop in an unplowed field, but just then the nose of the craft tilted up and there were no more bumps and jolts.

He twisted his head to the right and watched the ground drop away. The whole solar farm was spread out beneath them. Blinding flashes of light bounced off the polished mirrors of the bowl-shaped solar collectors.

"Electrical engineering may not be a glamour profession," Almonte said from the pilot's seat, "but it has its high points."

For the first time Frank realized that they didn't have to raise their voices over the drone of the engine. The electric motor made almost no noise. The only sound was the steady whir of the propeller cutting through the air.

"How fast are we going?" he asked.

Almonte nodded out the window. "Not fast enough to overtake any of those cars down there on the highway."

Frank looked down and saw that she was right. "How can you keep it in the air at such a low speed?"

"I told you it wasn't much more than an ultralite," she replied. "The stabilizer wing under the nose keeps the stall speed low, and we get some help from the thermal updrafts."

"Where'd you learn to fly?" Frank asked.

"You sure ask a lot of questions," she said. "Why don't you just relax and enjoy the ride?"

Frank opened his mouth to speak and then changed his mind. He decided to take her advice and settle back to admire the view. Up there, he could let his mind drift. It was so peaceful and quiet—almost too quiet, he told himself. He cocked his head and listened. He couldn't hear the propeller anymore.

But now he could hear Theresa softly talking to herself in front of him. "Trouble?" he asked, trying to sound untroubled.

"We lost power for a second," she told him. She punched the starter switch once, twice, three times. Nothing happened. She took off her helmet, unbuckled her shoulder harness, and stuck her head under the control panel. After fumbling with some wires for an endless minute, she tried the starter again.

She looked over her shoulder at Frank and smiled nervously. "Looks like we may be in for a rough landing. I can't get it—"

She never finished the sentence because a sudden downdraft threw the plane into a dive. The nose pitched down violently and Theresa Almonte's head was thrown forward, smashing into the controls.

Frank fought back the panic as her body slumped limply in the front seat. He was hurtling toward the ground in a flying coffin, with an unconscious pilot.

Chapter

4

FRANK DESPERATELY CLUTCHED the back of Theresa Almonte's shirt and struggled to pull her out of the pilot's seat. But the narrow cockpit and low canopy didn't leave him any room to maneuver.

Frank instantly knew there was only one chance. He leaned over the pilot's seat with outstretched hands, grasped the two canopy latches, and yanked them open.

The canopy flew back and snapped off. The wind blasted Frank in the face and whipped around the cockpit. He slapped the shoulder harness release and flung the straps out of his way. With both hands tightly gripping the pilot's seat, he hauled himself up and stuck one foot out onto the wing.

He took a deep breath. Now came the tough part. Straddling the lip of the cockpit and fighting against the stiff wind rushing past, he let go of the seat and grabbed the unconscious pilot with both hands. He managed to get her turned around and draped over the seat, her head and arms dangling down. Then he squirmed into the front cockpit and shoved Theresa Almonte into the backseat.

The ground was coming up fast. Frank seized the control yoke and pulled back as hard as he could. His back arched, and the muscles in his arms and neck bulged under the strain. Inch by painful inch the yoke yielded to Frank, and the plane started to pull out of its deadly descent.

Frank forced the control yoke back farther, and the plane finally leveled off. But it was almost skimming the treetops now, and the engine was dead. Frank didn't know if he could coax the plane back to the runway before the relentless tug of gravity dragged them down—but he didn't have much choice. He glanced over his shoulder at the woman crumpled in the backseat without a shoulder harness or helmet. He didn't want to think about what would happen to her in a crash landing.

The chain-link fence that surrounded the solar farm loomed ahead. It was going to be close. Frank grappled with the sluggish controls and managed to get the nose up a little. The front end of the plane cleared the fence. Then there was a thud, a clank, and the flimsy aircraft lurched upward.

Suddenly the plane was about twenty feet higher, and Frank needed every inch if he was to make the end of the runway. The plane hit the concrete hard and bounced twice before he got it under control again. It wasn't the best landing he had ever made, but none of the passengers complained.

Joe was already sprinting toward them before the plane rolled to a stop. He skidded to a halt when he saw his brother climb out of the pilot's seat. "I should have known you were driving when I saw the landing gear hit the top of the fence," he said. "It looked like you were trying to play leapfrog." He tried to sound nonchalant, as if it were no big deal, as if he watched his brother crash-land two or three crippled aircraft every day before breakfast.

But it was wasted effort. Frank didn't even notice how unfazed Joe pretended to be. He was too busy lifting Theresa Almonte out of the cockpit.

"Let me give you a hand," Joe said, climbing onto the wing. "What happened, anyway?"

"It's a long story," Frank replied.

Joe saw the haggard look on his brother's face and the purplish bruise on the woman's forehead. "Something tells me if it had been any longer, you wouldn't be here to tell it."

Almonte started to come around as Joe took

one of her arms and slung it over his shoulder "What's going on?" she asked in a shaky voice. "Where are we going?"

"To the nearest hospital," Frank told her. "You've got a pretty nasty bump on your head."

She raised a hand to her forehead. "Is that really necessary? I mean, is it really all that bad?"

"No," Joe responded. "It's not too bad. It's hardly any bigger than a regulation bowling ball." He guided her to her sports car, which was parked by the hangar.

"Give me your keys," he said. "I'm driving." He looked over at Frank. "Do you think you can handle the van by yourself?"

Frank thought that was a strange question. Then he realized that he probably looked pretty frazzled. "Don't worry," he assured his brother. "Right now I can handle just about anything— as long as it stays on the ground."

The Hardys hung around the hospital long enough to make sure Theresa was all right. Then they headed back to the solar farm.

"First Alec Ward, and now Theresa Almonte," Joe said as he steered the van down the highway. "Do you get the feeling somebody arranged for her to have a fatal accident?"

"I figure there are three possibilities," his brother replied. "The first is that it really was just an accident, and it's just an incredible coincidence that it happened the day after Ward's murder.''

"I wouldn't put a whole lot of money on that," Joe remarked. "It looks to me like somebody is trying to get rid of anybody who knows anything about the super solar cell."

"That's possibility number two," Frank said. "But why didn't they try to make Ward's death look like an accident, too?"

Joe knew the way his brother's mind worked. He didn't always get there as fast—but Joe usually reached the same conclusions sooner or later. "Possibility three—you think she rigged the plane herself?"

"I'm not ruling it out," Frank answered. "If everybody thinks the person who killed Ward is after Theresa now—presto, she's not a suspect anymore."

"Clever plan," Joe said. "She tries to kill herself to confuse the cops. Don't you think that's a fairly severe solution?"

"Not if smashing her head into the controls wasn't part of the plan," Frank argued. "That plane isn't much heavier than a glider. She could have landed it easily, even without power."

"Okay," Joe said as he stopped the van at the guard station outside the gate to the farm. "Let's say we find evidence of sabotage—how will we know who did it?"

"I can't answer that," Frank replied, "until I get a good look at the plane."

Joe rolled down his window and spoke to the guard. "Hi. Remember us? We were here earlier with Theresa Almonte."

"Sure," the guard said. "You were the ones who took her to the hospital. Is she all right?"

"She's fine," Joe answered. "We left some stuff in the hangar. Could you open the gate so we can go get it?"

The guard shook his head slowly. "Sorry. You're not authorized to be out here alone."

"We're not alone," Joe countered. "We're together."

"You know what I mean," the guard said.

Joe sighed. "Yeah, I do." He turned to his brother. "What now?"

Frank looked at his watch. "Now we go home."

Joe checked the mirror and backed the van out onto the road. "One quick phone call could have gotten us in," he muttered.

"And blown our cover," Frank added. "What is that guard going to think if he gets a call from the president of the company, telling him to let a couple of teenagers go anyplace they want? And who's going to hear him grumbling about it later?"

"You're right," Joe said simply, and let it go at that. Sometimes, Joe knew, it was better just to agree with Frank and drop a subject. Besides,

Frank was probably right, and Joe realized he was hungry. It was a good time to go home, anyway.

About an hour after dinner, Joe decided he needed something sweet. "Let's go and get some ice cream," he said. "I'll buy."

Frank was just about to listen to the messages on their answering machine but clicked it off when Joe spoke. "Can I get that in writing?"

Joe put his hand over his heart and staggered back. "You wound me. My own brother doesn't trust me."

Frank laughed. "I trust you, all right. I trust you to be broke all the time."

"It just so happens," Joe said smugly, reaching into his back pocket, "that I have—"

What he thought was in his back pocket wasn't there. He patted his front pockets. Not there either.

"Don't tell me you lost your wallet again," Frank said.

Joe slapped his forehead. "I left it in Theresa Almonte's car! It was that stupid parking lot at the hospital—the one where you have to pay to get in. I took my wallet out to get some money and then put it on the dashboard."

"And left it there," Frank said.

"I had a lot on my mind," Joe responded defensively.

"Don't worry about it," Frank told him. "You can get it tomorrow."

A smile appeared on Joe's face. "Why wait? This is a great excuse to check out where she lives."

He pulled out a telephone book and leafed through it, finally running a finger down one of the pages. "Here it is," he said. Then he tossed the book on the table and headed to the door. "Aren't you going to call her?" Frank asked.

Joe turned to his brother and grinned. "Let's surprise her instead."

The address in the phone book turned out to be that of a ranch house in a modest neighborhood. Only biting his tongue prevented Frank from saying "I told you so" when Joe got no answer to his repeated banging on the door.

"It was a good idea," Joe insisted as they climbed back into the van and pulled away from the curb.

A pair of headlights flashed across the front windshield, and a car moved slowly down the street. It pulled into the spot the van had occupied just a minute before. Joe cut the engine and watched two people coming out of a late model gray sedan. Joe saw that one of them was Theresa Almonte—and he recognized the other one, too.

"That's Ben Watson," he whispered as another set of headlights flashed in his eyes before being turned off.

Watson and Almonte stood on the sidewalk, talking for a minute. Even with the window down, Joe couldn't make out the words, though. They shook hands, and Watson slid back in his car and drove away.

Theresa Almonte was walking up the sidewalk to her house when Joe heard the muffled *whump* of a car door closing. He glanced in the direction of the noise and spotted a figure dressed in dark clothes moving quickly toward Theresa.

Before Frank realized what was happening, Joe bolted out the driver's side of the van and rushed at the figure. Now he could see that it was a man. The guy whipped around, and two cold, hard eyes locked on Joe.

The man's hand moved smoothly and swiftly inside his jacket pocket and came out again gripping an automatic pistol—aimed right at Joe's head.

Chapter

5

JOE ROARED and hurled himself headlong at the man with the gun, his eyes riveted on the dull black bore of the barrel. It looked huge, and Joe knew it could punch a hole the size of his fist.

These thoughts flashed through his mind in the split second it took him to close the gap between them. Joe's shoulder slammed into the man's chest, and they both toppled to the ground. There was a deafening blast, the pistol spitting fire and smoke.

Joe clutched the man's gun arm with both hands and smashed it down on the pavement. The weapon roared again. The sound of shattering glass followed by the high-pitched scream of a car alarm told Joe the second shot had gone wild.

A knee was driven up into Joe's stomach, knocking the wind out of him. A short "Oof!" forced its way past his lips as the air rushed out of his lungs. He fell back, gasping for breath while he struggled to hold on to the man's arm and pull himself up. Joe saw the leg swing up behind him in a blurred arc half a second before it hooked around his throat and jerked him backward again.

Joe tried to get up, but the man was on top of him in an instant, shoving the pistol barrel against his nose. It was cold and hard, just like the eyes glaring down at him.

"Give me a reason," a man rasped in a voice like ice. "So much as twitch the wrong way and I'll give you an extra nostril that'll let the air in from the other side. Just give me a reason."

"And give me a reason not to send you to dreamland," another voice growled. "Drop the gun and put your hands over your head."

Frank wielded the tire iron like a sledgehammer, hovering above the figure that crouched over his brother. He tapped the back of the man's head with the heavy metal rod. "Right now," he said simply.

The man pulled the pistol away from Joe's face and set it carefully on the sidewalk. Then he stood up slowly, hands raised high. Joe got his first good look at him. He was built like a small truck. Wide shoulders sloped up to a short, thick neck, merging into a bullet-shaped head that was completely bald, shaved clean from ear to ear. Joe thought he looked like a wrestler on TV.

"Frank? Joe?" Theresa Almonte stammered. "What is this? *Who* is this?"

"Do you know these gentlemen?" the bald man asked her.

"Yes," she said. "They work for me. But I don't know *you*."

"If you'll just let me get something out of my coat pocket," he replied, "I think it will explain everything."

Joe picked up the pistol and pointed it at him. "Go ahead, but make sure you don't even twitch in the wrong direction."

The man took out a folded sheet of paper and handed it to Theresa.

"What is it?" Frank asked.

"It's a note from John O'Hara," she said as she read. "He's Mike Barnes's silent money partner."

"Yeah, we know," Joe responded carelessly.

She stopped reading and glanced at him. "You two seem to know a lot."

"We just like to know who we work for," Frank said quickly. "And right now I'd like to know what's in that note that explains what this guy is doing here, waving guns around."

Theresa finished the note and smiled. "I think he was trying to protect me from you boys."

"That's correct," the man said. "My name is

45

Horace Sykes. I've been retained by Mr. O'Hara to provide personal protection for you, Ms. Almonte. I was coming to tell you now when I spotted this kid going up to intercept you."

Joe stared at him. "Personal protection?"

"A bodyguard," Frank said. "Why?"

"The note says it's just a precaution," Theresa explained. "Apparently, he thinks there's a chance that today's little incident may have been an attempt on my life."

"Little incident?" Joe responded. "You mean the plane? How'd he find out about that?"

Theresa shrugged. "There's not a lot that goes on at Bright Futures that John O'Hara doesn't know about."

Frank was about to ask Sykes for some kind of identification when the guys who do that for a living started to show up. Gunshots on a sleepy Bayport street tended to attract a lot of blue lights and uniforms to match.

The two-way radio in the squad car squawked behind him as Con Riley hitched up his gun belt and strolled over to the Hardys. Riley's eyes moved from Frank to Joe and back again. "Why aren't I surprised to find you here?"

By the time Frank, Joe, Theresa Almonte, and Horace Sykes finished explaining the whole silly misunderstanding, Chief Collig showed up, and they had to start again from the beginning. The sour expression on Collig's face never changed.

Joe decided he probably practiced by sucking lemons in front of a mirror.

"So you just came by to get your wallet, is that it?" the police chief cut in when he had heard enough.

Joe and Frank both nodded.

"Then get it and go," Collig said tersely. He turned to Con Riley. "What about this Sykes character—does he check out?"

"Right down the line," Riley said. "His gun permit's up to date, his record is clean, and I just got information from O'Hara that Sykes is working for him. By the way, boys, O'Hara says he left a message on your answering machine, telling you about Sykes here. Maybe you'd better listen to it once in a while."

The police chief glared at the Hardys. "Why are you still here?"

Theresa Almonte grabbed Joe's arm. "Come on," she said. "My car's over there. Let's see if your wallet's in it."

"Good idea," Frank chimed in. "I'll go with you."

Theresa unlocked the car door and found Joe's wallet on the dashboard. "I don't know how I missed it when I drove home from the hospital," she said, handing the wallet to Joe. "I guess my mind was somewhere else."

"Maybe you were thinking about your date tonight," Frank ventured.

She gave him a curious look. "Date?"

Frank shifted into his best imitation of a teen-ager—or at least what most adults think of as a teenager. "Well, I mean, we saw that guy drop you off. I guess I just *assumed* he was your boy-friend or something. I mean, hey, it's none of my business."

Her face hardened. "You're right," she replied sharply. "It's none of your business." She spun on her heel and took a half dozen steps before stopping and turning around. "I'm sorry. I didn't mean to bite your head off. It's been a long day, you know?"

"It sure has," Frank agreed.

Theresa sighed wearily. "You guys really put yourselves on the line for me today, so I guess I owe you some kind of explanation."

"You don't owe us anything," Joe said.

"Maybe I owe it to myself," she replied. "I'll feel better if I get it off my chest. You see, that man I was with offered me a lot of money to come work for him."

"What's wrong with that?" Frank asked.

She shrugged and smiled weakly. "Maybe nothing."

Con Riley walked up and nodded toward the Hardys' black van. "I've been instructed to escort you gentlemen to your vehicle."

"Oh, boy," Joe said. "I always wanted a police escort."

"I'm sorry about this," Riley said as the three

of them walked to the van. "But this murder investigation has the chief on edge."

"How's it going?" Frank prodded. "Did forensics turn up anything you can use?"

"Not much," Riley replied. "There were traces of acid mixed in with the bloodstains on the carpet. The last I heard, they were still identifying it."

"Anything else?" Frank pressed.

Riley eyed him warily. "Why do I have the feeling I've told you too much already?"

Frank smiled and opened the van door. "Don't worry about it. You know me—I'm just the curious type."

"Yes," Riley replied soberly. "I do know you—and that's why I'm worried."

It had been a long night, so Joe slept late the next morning. It was Saturday, and since he couldn't come up with any particular reason to get out of bed, he stayed there as long as possible.

His aunt Gertrude finally rousted him a little after ten. "Chet Morton is here," she said, opening Joe's curtains and letting the sun stream in. "He called earlier, and I told him I was sure you'd be up by now."

"Yeah, right," Joe mumbled, squinting against the light. "Where's Frank?"

"He's busy with that computer of his," Gertrude said, "and I just hate to disturb him when he's working."

Joe studied his aunt standing there, smiling benignly. "Okay," he said. "I get the hint. Tell Chet I'll be right down."

Joe stumbled down the stairs a few minutes later and found Chet in the kitchen, indulging in his favorite pastime.

"Hi, Joe," Chet managed to say around a mouthful of food. He was holding a half-eaten sandwich of some kind.

"A little early for lunch, isn't it?" Joe remarked.

Chet chewed thoughtfully for a moment and swallowed. "Your aunt was so insistent. It would have been rude to say no."

Joe laughed. "It would have been a *miracle*." Chet had the wide, massive frame of a football linebacker—but the only sport he took a lot of interest in was marathon eating.

"Hey, Chet," Frank called from behind Joe. "What's up?"

Frank walked into the kitchen and glanced at his brother. "And what got you out of bed before noon?"

"Give me a break," Joe responded. "I worked pretty hard the last couple of days."

"Yeah," Chet said. "That's what I wanted to talk to you guys about. Your aunt told me you got part-time jobs at that solar energy company."

"So much for our cover," Joe muttered.

Chet's eyes widened. "You're on a case?" A slight frown creased his forehead. "Oh, then I guess you can't help me out."

"What's the problem?" Frank asked.

"Well," Chet said, "I really need an after-school job right now, and I thought maybe they were looking for more part-time guys where you work."

Joe shook his head. "Sorry, Chet. Anyway, I don't think you want to get too close to solar energy right now. It seems to have developed lethal side effects."

"Wait a minute," Frank said. He looked at Chet. "You can type, right?"

Chet nodded.

Frank smiled. "Then I've got the perfect job for you—and you just might be able to help us with our case."

"I'm afraid you might not have a case anymore."

Frank and Joe turned to see their father standing in the kitchen door.

"I just got a call from John O'Hara," he told them. "Theresa Almonte's been arrested for industrial espionage—and the murder of Alec Ward."

Chapter

6

FRANK STARED at his father. "What do they have on her?"

"I wouldn't call it an airtight case," Fenton Hardy answered, "but it doesn't look good for her, either. The security guards caught her leaving the Bright Futures offices early this morning with copies of part of the plans for the super cell. After they contacted the police, the police got a warrant and searched her house. They found some working notes in her desk in what appears to be Alec Ward's handwriting."

"Is that all?" Frank asked.

"Not quite," his father said. "The notes were spattered with dried blood—Alec Ward's blood type. She could have taken them off the body after she killed him."

Joe rubbed his eyes and shook the last of the sleep out of his head. "All that happened this morning? A guy can't close his eyes for ten minutes around here."

Frank checked his watch. "Ten hours is more like it. Where is Theresa now? Can we see her?"

Fenton Hardy shrugged. "She could be back home by now—if she has a good lawyer. She doesn't have an arrest record, and there's probably not enough evidence to charge her."

Frank looked over at his brother. "Come on, we've got work to do."

"I wish I did, too," Chet said glumly.

"You do," Frank replied. "You're going to apply for a part-time job at Solex, Inc."

Chet groaned. "I am? On Saturday?"

"Sure," Frank said. "It shows initiative and drive. They'll love it."

This time when Joe knocked at the door of the modest ranch house, there was an answer. The fact that Frank had called first to make sure somebody was there might have helped—but Joe didn't expend much energy on trivial details.

"I don't know why I agreed to see you," Theresa Almonte said as she opened the door and waved to Sykes, who was sitting in his car. She led the Hardys into a small study, where every available space was covered with a jumbled assortment of books, magazines, and loose sheets of paper.

Joe pushed a pile of books off to one side of a well-worn couch and sat down. Frank found a step stool next to a floor-to-ceiling bookcase and sat on it.

Almonte leaned against her cluttered desk, her arms crossed, a guarded look on her face. "My life has fallen apart completely since I met you. Now you call and show up on my doorstep only a half hour after I get out of jail.

"Something tells me your real job doesn't have a thing to do with being my assistants," she continued. "So before we go any further, tell me why I should be talking to you at all."

"Because we might be able to help you," Frank replied. *"If* you're innocent."

"I'm listening," Almonte said tersely. "Keep going."

The two brothers exchanged sidelong glances. Joe raised his eyebrows and shrugged his shoulders, wordlessly saying, "Why not?"

Frank decided it was time for a little truth. "We were hired to check out the security at Bright Futures," he explained. "Until we're sure of what happened—until we have proof—we haven't finished our job."

"So what do you want from me?" Theresa snapped. "A confession?"

"No," Frank said. "We want the truth."

"Okay," she replied. "I'll tell you the same thing I told the police. I didn't kill Alec, and I don't know who did. I don't know how his notes

54

got in my house, and I don't know where those papers came from that the security guards pulled out of my purse at the office."

"They searched your purse?" Joe asked.

Almonte nodded. "They've been doing random checks of bags and briefcases for a while now. On a slow day like Saturday, they tend to give everybody the full treatment on the way out."

"That makes sense," Frank said. "But what were you doing in the office on a Saturday?"

"I didn't know working on the weekend was a crime," she retorted. "And if it is, go arrest Mike Barnes. He's there seven days a week—and he gets cranky if Tom and I don't put in at least a six-day week."

"Tom Kilman?" Frank verified.

Joe had been wandering around the cluttered room, but he stopped when he heard Kilman's name. Kilman the reptile, was how Joe thought of him. Bet he hadn't even evolved to being warm-blooded yet, Joe decided. "Kilman was working today, too?" he asked.

"If Mike works, Tom works," she answered.

"Is this where they found Ward's notes?" Frank asked, pointing to the desk.

"Yes," Theresa said. She started to move around, picking up loose papers and piling them in stacks. "I know I'm never going to win any Good Housekeeping awards, but this wasn't quite such a disaster area before the police plowed through it.''

Joe smiled. ''That's one of their specialties.'' He pushed himself up off the couch. ''Mind if we look around?''

''Mind if I ask why?'' she responded.

''If somebody planted those notes,'' Frank explained, ''they had to get in the house. Any evidence of a break-in would help your story.''

Theresa sighed and gestured to the door. ''Go ahead. I'm getting used to complete strangers nosing around my home.''

It didn't take Frank and Joe long to check out the other four rooms in the small house. Joe tested all the windows, and Frank examined the front and back doors before they went outside.

''It doesn't look like anybody forced either of the doors,'' Frank told his brother as they walked out to the backyard.

''No one would have to,'' Joe responded. ''There isn't a single window that can't be reached easily from the ground—unless you're a dwarf.''

''How about a dwarf with a ladder?'' Frank countered. ''What's your point?''

Joe nodded toward a window. ''That bedroom window over there isn't locked.''

Joe stepped up to the window. There was no place to get a good grip on it, so he had to place his flattened palms against the glass pane and push. The window didn't budge.

Frank picked up a stick and handed it to him. "Here, try this."

"What am I supposed to do with this? Break the glass?"

"Do you see any broken glass?" Frank responded.

"No," Joe said in a slightly annoyed tone. "I was trying to do it without breaking the glass."

"Right," Frank said, grabbing the stick. "Look, the pane isn't flush against the window—it's set into it. The putty that holds it in place forms a little lip all the way around." He took the stick, jammed it up against the lip at the top of the lower window and gave it a firm push.

The window moved up a few inches. Frank glanced back over his shoulder at Joe. "You get a lot more leverage that way." He worked his hands into the space at the bottom and forced the window open wide enough to crawl through. He gripped the sill, hauled himself up, and wriggled inside. Then he peered back out at Joe, a smug smile on his face.

Joe responded by grabbing the bottom of the window and slamming it shut.

Frank opened it again and stuck his head out. "Why'd you do that?"

"Climb back out here," Joe said, "and I'll show you."

"This better not be one of your stupid tricks," Frank grumbled as he clambered over the sill and dropped to the ground.

"It's not," Joe said. He pulled the window down and pointed. "The putty is still a little soft," he explained. "So there's a mark—a kind of dent—where you pressed the stick against it. See?"

Frank looked more closely and saw two dent marks in the putty. He glanced over at his brother. "Do you know what this means?"

It was Joe's turn to smile. "Sure. It means we should start looking for a dwarf with a ladder and a stick."

A half hour later the black van pulled into the Bright Futures parking lot.

"What are we looking for?" Joe asked Frank as they walked into the office where they had met Alec Ward for the first and last time.

Frank shrugged his shoulders. "Beats me. Anything that might tell us who killed Ward and why that person wants to frame Theresa Almonte."

Joe sat down at the desk and opened a file cabinet drawer. "She didn't go to Alec's apartment to check on him, remember. She asked us to go—so we found the body. How can you be sure it's a frame job?"

"I'm not," Frank admitted. "But she seems too bright to stuff company secrets in her purse and try to smuggle them past the guard. Especially when she knew they made thorough searches on Saturday. It just doesn't figure.

You'd think she'd be a little more inventive, wouldn't you?''

Joe nodded as he scanned the color-coordinated, alphabetical file folders. He looked under C for clues, but didn't find anything. "I also think this is a waste of time. We should be searching his apartment, not his office.''

"Until the police seal comes off the door, that's going to be a little tricky," Frank reminded him. "They may even have a twenty-four–hour guard on the place.''

Joe waved his hand around the tidy work space. Neat rows of technical manuals lined the shelves on the wall. "Look at how meticulous this place is. If we find a book that isn't filed under the correct subject heading, we should haul it downtown for questioning.''

He stood up and reached for one of the books, but he forgot that he hadn't closed the cabinet and banged his shin against it. He hopped backward, clutching at his leg, and bumped into the telephone, knocking it off the desk.

The phone crashed to the floor and landed on its side. When Joe bent down to pick it up, he spotted something taped to the bottom. "Hey, what do we have here?" he wondered out loud.

Joe palmed the small, round, metallic device and held it out for his brother to see. He looked up and saw a man with a gray beard and a sharp nose standing in the doorway.

"Oh, hi, Mr. O'Hara," Joe said uneasily. "I thought you were in New York."

"I always come in on Saturdays. Find anything interesting?" O'Hara asked.

Frank reached over and plucked the object out of Joe's hand. He inspected it quickly and then showed it to O'Hara. "Is it routine security around here to bug the phones?"

The color drained from the older man's face. "The phones are tapped?"

"This is the only one we know about," Frank said.

"We should tell the police right away," O'Hara responded. He held out his hand. "Give it to me. I'll take care of it."

Frank's fingers closed around the device. "We'll contact them ourselves."

"All right," O'Hara said stiffly. "Well, we better have security check all the phones. I'll go tell Mike." He headed off down the hall at a brisk pace.

Frank called Con Riley and told him about the bug and the forced window.

"That was interesting," he said afterward. "Let's see what else we can find."

Joe groaned. "Don't tell me you want to go through all his files."

Frank checked out the computer equipment before his eyes rested on a fat metal box with a slot in the front. "That could take a very long time," he replied. He ran his hand lightly over the top of the box. "This is an optical disk drive." He tapped a small stack of thin plastic cases on the desk. "And these are the disks."

"They look like compact disk cases," Joe remarked.

"They are," Frank said. "Only these disks each carry three hundred megabytes of information."

Joe did some rough math in his head. "Three hundred million bytes? That's 150,000 pages apiece! It could take years to go through all that!"

Frank put his arm around his brother and steered him toward the door. "That's why we're not going to do it—not yet, anyway, and if we do, we'll ask Theresa to help us."

Outside, it was easy to spot the van in the nearly deserted parking lot. "Not everybody works on the weekends," Joe observed as he climbed into the driver's seat.

"No," Frank said, "but Theresa Almonte wasn't the only one in the office today, either. We know Tom and Mike and O'Hara were here, too."

"True," Joe conceded. He started the engine and pulled out of the parking space. Turning out of the parking lot, Joe punched the gas pedal as he pulled onto the street.

"What's the big hurry?" Frank asked.

"We always get stuck at that stoplight up there," Joe said. "But if I time it just right—"

The light turned yellow.

"I'm not getting stuck this time," Joe muttered to the light. He pressed his foot down harder.

"You won't make it," Frank said. "Come on, this is really dangerous."

Joe realized his brother was right. He lifted his foot off the gas and pushed down on the brake pedal.

The van didn't slow.

"You're not going to make it!" Frank yelled.

Joe pumped the brake pedal frantically. There didn't seem to be any pressure. "The brakes are gone!" he shouted. "I can't stop!"

The light turned red. The van sped into the intersection, out of control.

Chapter

7

JOE BLASTED THE HORN in a desperate attempt to keep traffic out of the intersection, but it was already too late. A car had shot out in front of the runaway van, and Joe had to crank the wheel hard to swerve around it. The top-heavy van rocked from side to side as Joe jerked the wheel back the other way, barely making it past the front bumper of a pickup truck.

Then they were across the intersection—but it wasn't over yet. The traffic up ahead was slowed to a crawl, and Joe had about ten seconds to do something before the van rear-ended the last car in the long line, which would start a deadly chain reaction.

"Use the emergency brake!" Frank shouted.

Joe leaned over and grabbed the release lever with his left hand. He had to keep it pulled out while his left foot pressed down on the small pedal. If he didn't, the emergency break would lock up.

There was a sharp screech of metal while the emergency brake tried to do what it was never intended to do—actually stop a vehicle. The only "emergency" it was designed for was parking on a hill.

Then the cable snapped, and the van had no brakes of any kind.

Joe's right hand found the shift and slammed it into low gear. The van lurched and did slow down abruptly, but it was still on a collision course with a license plate that Joe could almost reach out and touch.

He clutched the wheel and steered the van to the curb. The right front tire scraped the curb. Joe turned the wheel a little to the left to back off some, then nudged the curb again, using it like a cement brake. Each time the tire nosed the curb, the speedometer dipped further down.

Finally the van idled to a complete stop.

Joe waited a few seconds, half expecting some car to smash into the back of the van. When nothing happened, he took a deep breath and pried his fingers off the steering wheel.

"That's the last time I try to run a yellow light," he said, holding up his right hand. "I promise."

"Don't make promises you can't keep," Frank said. He reached into his front pocket and pulled out a dime. "Call it—heads or tails," he said as he flipped the coin in the air.

"Uh, heads," Joe responded right after he saw the dime drop back into Frank's palm, heads up.

Frank smiled. "Looks like you win."

"Great," Joe replied. "What do I win?"

"You get to crawl under the van and look at the brakes," Frank told him.

Joe frowned. "How about two out of three?" he suggested.

Frank shook his head. "No, no. You won fair and square." He opened his door and hopped out. "Get out on this side," he said. "We wouldn't want to get hit by a truck before you can collect your prize."

"With my luck," Joe grumbled as he slid across the seat and climbed out of the van, "I'll get hit by a truck *after* I collect my prize."

"Don't forget this," Frank said cheerfully, handing him the flashlight from the glove compartment.

Joe got a piece of wood from the back of the van and put it in front of the rear wheels to lock them in place before he lay down on his back and worked his way under the front of the van. He shone the flashlight up at the hoses and wires that snaked around the engine. It didn't take long to spot the problem.

"I found it!" he called out.

Frank crouched down and peered under the van. "What is it?"

"You can't see it from there," Joe said.

"Then why don't you just tell me what it is?" Frank suggested.

"No," Joe replied. "I think this requires your keen investigative eye."

Frank sighed. "You're not going to tell me, are you?"

"Nope."

"I'm going to have to crawl under there to find out, right?"

"That's right."

"Okay," Frank said as he wriggled in next to his brother on the grimy pavement.

Joe played the flashlight beam along the brake line. A few drops of fluid glistened in the light, dangling from the spot where the line had been cleanly severed.

"No brake fluid, no brakes," Joe said. "It's as simple as that."

Frank ran a finger over the smooth edge of the cut. "The hard part is finding out who did it—and why."

Between them, Frank and Joe had just enough money to have the van towed and repaired at a nearby service station.

"Looks like somebody doesn't like you boys too much," the mechanic remarked as he wiped his greasy hands with an even greasier rag. "There's no way that was an accident—unless some guy holding a knife tripped and fell under there and kind of poked the brake line by mistake.''

"That's probably exactly what happened," Joe said.

The mechanic grunted. "All the same, I'd watch my back if I were you."

"We will," Frank said. "Believe me, we will."

There wasn't much daylight left when the black van pulled up next to the space where it had been parked a few hours earlier. But Frank and Joe didn't have much trouble making out the dark blotch where the brake fluid had soaked into the blacktop.

"It happened right here," Frank said.

Joe nodded. "While we were in Ward's office, somebody was out here practicing his whittling on our brake line."

Frank started to walk toward the office building. "Let's find out who was working today."

"How are we going to do that?" Joe responded. "Just go up to the security desk and ask?"

Frank stopped at the revolving glass door and smiled over his shoulder at his brother. "Something like that," he said.

Joe seriously considered sitting this one out, but his curiosity got the better of him. He caught up with Frank just as he reached the security desk.

"Excuse me," Frank said, showing the guard his photo ID. "This may sound silly, but I think I forgot to sign out when I left this afternoon."

The guard scowled. "Nobody gets past this desk without signing out."

"I know," Frank said. "But I drove all the way back here just to make sure. I mean, I didn't want you guys to spend half the night searching the place for me, so couldn't I just check the log?"

"All right," the guard said gruffly. He opened the log book and ran his finger down the column of names. There weren't enough entries for the day to fill a page. "Here it is," he said smugly. "Frank Hardy. You came in at two-thirty and left at three-fifteen. I told you no one leaves without signing the log."

Frank scratched his head. "It says three-fifteen? That can't be right, can it?"

The guard spun the book around on the table and shoved it at him. "Here! See for yourself."

Frank quickly scanned the list of names and times. "You're absolutely right," he said after double-checking the list. "Sorry to have wasted your time."

The guard just glared at him.

Joe flashed his warmest smile and tugged at his brother's arm as they backed away from the desk. "Well, thanks for all your help. We'll just get out of here and let you get back to whatever it is you do."

Joe could still feel the guard's eyes boring into his back when they got outside.

"So what did you find out?" he finally asked when the van was on the road again.

"Three people left the office after two-thirty and before three-fifteen," Frank told him. "One of them was John O'Hara."

Joe raised his eyebrows. "You think our own client is trying to put us in the morgue next to Alec Ward?"

"I don't think anybody tried to kill us," Frank answered. "That brake job was meant to rattle us, maybe scare us off the case."

"What makes you think that?" Joe asked.

"Two reasons," Frank replied. "Number one— a runaway vehicle isn't a very reliable murder weapon. The odds of a fatal crash are pretty low."

"But what if we were on a steep mountain road?" Joe countered.

Frank gestured out the window. "Do you see any mountains?"

"No," Joe said. "But there's the cliff road by the bay."

"Yes," Frank agreed. "But first you'd have to get to the cliff road, which brings me to reason number two. The brake line was cut cleanly and completely. No slow leaks, no attempt to make it look like anything other than a deliberate act. There was zero fluid in the lines before you even started the engine. It was dumb luck that we got out of the parking lot at all."

"I hadn't thought of that," Joe said. "So we were just supposed to sort of drift into a lamp post or a parked car or something, get scared, and run away. Is that the idea?"

"It looks that way," Frank said. Joe frowned. "But why would O'Hara bother with all that? If he wanted us off the case, he could just fire us."

"Not if he didn't want us to know he wanted us off the case," Frank pointed out. "And don't forget—two other people could have sabotaged the van on their way out."

"I forgot about that," Joe said. "Anybody we know?"

Frank nodded. "Tom Kilman signed out at 3:05—just a few minutes after we had our little encounter with John O'Hara."

"That's one," Joe said. "Who's the other one?"

"None other than Mike Barnes himself."

Joe studied his brother. "You don't suspect Barnes, do you?"

"At this point," Frank replied, "I suspect everybody."

Chapter

8

JOE ATTEMPTED TO SLEEP LATE again the next morning, but Frank had other plans for him. Frank also knew the right buttons to push to get Joe moving.

"Wake up," Frank said, prodding the lump under the covers. "We'll be late for school."

A hand slid out of the lump and pulled the blanket back just far enough to reveal a patch of blond hair, part of a forehead, and one half-open eye. "Whutimezit?" a voice remotely like Joe's mumbled.

"Time for breakfast," Frank told him. "It's already on the table. Hurry up."

The lump struggled to something resembling a sitting position, and the covers fell away. Joe stretched and yawned. "Breakfast? Where am

I? I mean, where is it? No, I mean, what is it?''

"The meal before lunch," Frank answered.

"I know that," Joe said as he ran a hand through his tangled hair. It felt as if it had crazy spikes sticking out at weird angles. He made a mental note not to look in the mirror when he got dressed. "What I mean is—I forget what I mean. Never mind. I'll be down in ten minutes."

"Make it five," Frank said, throwing a pair of jeans into his brother's lap.

Joe got dressed and made his way downstairs on automatic pilot. He wasn't even sure how he got to the kitchen, but there he was—and there was Frank, sitting at the table.

Joe looked around. "Where is everybody? Where's breakfast?"

"In bed, and right here," Frank replied, tapping a box on a table.

"That's a box of cereal," Joe observed.

Frank nodded. "That's right."

Joe stared at the box. "That's it? That's breakfast?" The fog in his brain started to clear. "Wait a minute—it's Sunday!"

He glanced at the clock on the wall over the stove. "And it's not even seven o'clock!"

Frank smiled. "That's three for three. I keep telling people you're not nearly as stupid as you look."

Joe slumped down in a chair. He knew he should be angry, but it took too much energy.

"Oh, well," he said. "Now that I'm here, you might as well get me a bowl and some milk—and stay out of my way for the next fifteen minutes."

Joe could polish off a bowl of cereal in about two minutes—but not that day. That morning he was going to linger over every spoonful, savor every bite, chew every flake into a million tiny fragments, and drive Frank up the wall.

His plan worked brilliantly, right up to the point where their father came through the door. He was wearing a sleeveless mesh shirt, nylon running shorts, and a pair of running shoes that looked as if they had been designed for astronauts to wear on Mars. There was a thick sheen of sweat on his face.

"Nothing like a quick five-mile run to get a jump-start on the day," he said cheerfully. He wasn't even breathing heavily.

Frank promptly forgot about Joe's attempt to set the world record for the longest breakfast consisting of a single serving of cereal. "Any word yet on that phone bug?" he asked his father.

"It's Sunday, Frank," Fenton Hardy replied. "And it's not even seven o'clock."

Joe set his spoon down in the soggy flakes floating in lukewarm milk. "That's what *I* said."

"I just thought I'd ask," Frank said a little defensively. "It could help us break this case."

Fenton Hardy put his hand on his older son's shoulder. "I know. That's why I took it in to the station right after you gave it to me. I also took a good look at it myself and made a few calls."

Frank's eyes lit up. "Then you *do* know something."

"I know it's not an off-the-shelf piece of surveillance equipment," his father said.

Frank knew that his father knew what he was talking about. As a former police officer and detective, Fenton Hardy was no stranger to electronic bugging devices.

"It was either handmade or extensively modified," Fenton explained.

"So we're dealing with a pro," Joe said.

"If the phone tap was done by a pro," Frank asked, "do you think Ward's murder was a contract hit?"

"I never ran across a hitman who clubbed his victims to death," Fenton Hardy answered. "Guys that kill for a living usually prefer a small-caliber handgun at close range. It's easy to conceal, doesn't make a lot of noise, and does the job quickly and efficiently.

"Besides," he added, "if I thought a professional killer was involved, I'd yank you off the case and notify the organized crime division of the FBI.

"Furthermore," he said in a stern voice, "your job is to check out security at Bright Futures—not investigate the murder of Alec

Ward." His eyes locked on Frank. "Are we clear on that?"

Joe decided that was his cue to get up from the table. "As a matter of fact, we were just on our way out to do that very thing. Check security, that is."

"It's Sunday," his father reminded him.

"Right," Frank replied. "What better day to check security? Catch them off guard. See how good they really are."

Fenton Hardy sighed. "I don't know how you two talked me into letting you handle this case in the first place. Get out of here before I regain my sanity."

Joe didn't ask where they were going; he just let Frank drive, and waited for his brother to tell him or show him what he had in mind.

It didn't take long for Joe to figure out that what they had told their father wasn't all that far from the truth. "How nice," he said as he gazed out at the pastures and fields. "A drive in the country on Sunday morning."

Frank smiled and pulled the van over to the side of the road beside a familiar chain-link fence. "This looks like a nice spot to take a stroll."

They both got out of the van. Frank walked around to the rear door and unlocked it. He reached inside and pulled out the mat that covered the floor.

"Good idea," Joe remarked when he saw what Frank was holding in his hands.

Joe glanced around to make sure no cars were in sight. Then, without another word, he grasped the metal links with both hands and started climbing the fence. He stopped near the top, where razor-sharp barbed wire jutted outward. With the toes of his sneakers wedged in the steel mesh, and the fingers of his left hand wrapped around it, he reached back with his free hand to take the mat from Frank.

Joe swung the mat up and over the top of the fence, draping it over the coils of barbed wire. Then he gave it a hard tug. Jagged metal teeth sank into the fabric, holding it firmly in place.

"Now look what you've done," Frank said. "We'll probably have to climb over to the other side to get it off there."

"Gee," Joe replied with a grin, "do you think anybody will mind?"

Frank joined his brother on the fence. "Not if we do it fast," he whispered. He scrambled over the mat and dropped down to the ground on the other side.

Joe was right behind him, and two minutes later the two brothers reached the small forest of bowl-shaped collectors on the outskirts of the solar farm.

Frank stopped to take a close look at one. It was mounted on a circular platform. He had to stand on his tiptoes to see over the lower edge of the tilted bowl. The concave surface was lined with polished mirrors. In the center was a rectangular grid of flat black solar cells.

Joe peered over his brother's shoulder. "Just fill it with water and you've got a solar hot tub big enough for the whole family. We could sell a million of them in California."

Frank reached down into the bowl with his outstretched arm, careful not to touch the surface. He could feel the intense, radiated heat of the sun, bouncing off the mirrors, directed at the array of solar cells in the center. "You might have a hard time keeping it filled," he replied.

"Why?" Joe asked.

Frank pulled his arm out of the bowl and touched his brother's cheek. Joe flinched with surprise at the warmth in Frank's fingers. "Because," Frank said, "something tells me it'll crank enough power to vaporize a whole swimming pool full of water."

As they walked away, Joe had the eerie feeling that the solar collectors were watching them. He glanced back nervously and then tapped his brother on the shoulder. "Uh, don't look now, but I think those things are moving."

"They are moving," Frank said calmly. "They're turning to follow the sun as it moves across the sky. There's an electric motor in the base of each platform."

"Are you sure?" Joe asked doubtfully. "I mean, how do you know all that?"

"I did a little homework," Frank replied. "While you were testing your mattress for long-distance durability yesterday morning, I was using the computer to get some information on Bright Futures."

Joe looked at his brother. "Learn anything else that I should know about?"

"I'll tell you later," Frank said. He nodded toward the airplane hangar a distance away. "First, let's see what we can learn in there."

They quickly scouted the area. There were several cars parked by the other two buildings, but none near the hangar. The guard in the booth by the gate had his back to the Hardys, and there was nobody else outside.

They strolled casually up to the hangar door, acting as if they had every right to be there. It might be enough to fool the guard if he happened to glance their way. Frank was prepared to pick the lock, but he didn't have to. The door was open—just a crack, but open.

As he pushed the door open, the lights inside clicked off, leaving him in cool darkness. Frank crouched down low, grabbing Joe's arm to yank him down as he entered.

As Frank groped along the wall trying to find a light switch, something slammed into him, knocking him off his feet.

A figure bolted out the door.

Frank lay there, gasping, the wind knocked

out of him. "Get him," he managed to stammer out to his brother.

Joe sprinted out into the sunlight and instantly spotted a man in a business suit running far ahead of him across the field, heading for the bowl-shaped solar collectors.

Joe took off after him, knowing he could overtake the man. He quickly narrowed the distance between them, but the figure disappeared in the maze of solar collectors before Joe could catch up.

Joe plunged in after him, but he had lost sight of his target and had to stop and look around. He cocked his head and listened. The eerie feeling of being watched crept over him as he listened to the hum of an electric motor behind him.

Joe whirled around and was hit by an intense flash of light. He threw up his hands to shield his eyes. A searing heat scorched his forearms.

There was a thunderous blast—followed by ominous silence.

Chapter
9

FRANK HAD MADE HIS WAY out of the hangar just as Joe dashed into the middle of the solar collectors. Then he heard the blast and spotted a column of black smoke curling skyward.

A figure ran out of the cluster of shiny, bowl-shaped objects—but it wasn't Joe. Frank did get a good look at his face. It was Mike Barnes's assistant, Tom Kilman, and he was heading for one of the small buildings. Frank knew he could cut him off, but there was still no sign of Joe. He had to make a choice—go after Kilman or find his brother.

There really wasn't any choice at all.

Frank ran toward the dark, billowing cloud of smoke rising from the ground. It felt as if some-one was stabbing him with a knife every time he had to take a deep breath, but if Joe were hurt, every second counted. Frank was painfully aware of each one ticking by as he pushed himself across the field.

He found Joe lying facedown, a few feet from the smoldering remains of one of the large solar collectors. Kneeling down beside him, Frank put two fingers on the side of his brother's neck and felt a strong pulse. Joe stirred and let out a low groan.

"Where's the ball?" Joe mumbled as he tried to push himself off the ground. "Did I get the first down?"

"Take it slow and easy," Frank said, putting a hand on his brother's shoulder. "Does anything feel broken?"

Joe blinked and gazed at him. "I don't think so," he replied slowly, trying to remember where he was and what he was doing there.

"How about your head?" Frank asked.

Joe frowned. "Does it look broken?"

"No," Frank said patiently. "Do you feel dizzy or anything?"

Joe shook his head. The movement made him dizzy. "Only when I shake my head," he responded.

It all started to come back to him. He looked past his brother at the burnt-out shell of the solar collector. "You were right about the hot-tub idea," he said, rubbing the singed hair on his forearm. "It would never work out. But I think we should definitely look into the barbecue angle."

Frank wasn't the only one who had seen or

heard the blast. The uniformed guard from the front gate was on the scene quickly. The Hardys flashed their ID cards, and for the moment that seemed to satisfy him. But before it occurred to him to ask them just how they got there in the first place, the familiar, round form of Mike Barnes appeared. He glanced at Joe and then turned to the guard. "Aren't you going to call an ambulance?"

"Y-yes, sir," the guard sputtered. "I'm sorry, I didn't know anybody was here, sir."

"Well, go and do it now," Barnes ordered.

"I'm all right," Joe insisted, finally managing to stand on his own. "I was just kind of dazed for a few minutes, that's all."

Barnes studied the two brothers for a moment. Then his attention shifted to the charred round dish. "Well, you two have certainly had a busy morning," he said dryly. "What are you doing here, anyway?"

"Chasing bad guys," Joe answered.

Barnes smiled thinly. "Care to elaborate? I'm not in the mood for games. I just watched a large pile of money go up in smoke."

"You may lose more," Frank told him, "if you don't do something about Tom Kilman."

The round man's eyebrows arched up. "What does Tom have to do with this?"

"We caught him in your hangar with your solar plane," Frank replied. "And he didn't want to be seen in there."

"Do you think he was trying to steal solar cells?" Barnes asked.

Frank shrugged. "Maybe, but another possibility is that he was removing evidence."

"But what evidence could he try to remove—the police checked out the plane already," Barnes said.

"I don't know," Frank replied evenly. "All I know is that one of your two top engineers is dead, the other was almost killed, and your assistant was in your hangar near the plane that almost killed her. He obviously didn't want to be seen in there or he wouldn't have run."

"Don't forget that he tried to fry me with that solar gizmo," Joe added.

Barnes silently studied the boys. "So, you don't believe Theresa killed Alec and then set up the attempt on herself?"

Frank and Joe exchanged a quick glance before shaking their heads in unison.

"But what about the evidence the police found at her house?" Barnes asked, not really expecting an answer. He turned his head to take in the approach of another man.

He looked like a serious body-builder to Frank. The jacket he wore didn't hide his wide shoulders or muscular neck. He walked ramrod straight, like a soldier, and Frank could clearly see the bulge of a shoulder holster under the jacket. He stopped a few yards away.

"You can go," Barnes said to him.

"I don't think that's a good idea, Mr. Barnes," the man responded. "You've already slipped away from me once today. I can't protect you if I don't know where you are."

Barnes sighed. "All right, Norbert. You win."

"So you got a bodyguard, too," Frank said.

"Just today. Another of O'Hara's ideas," Barnes replied. "He's a nuisance, but at least I always know where he is and what he's doing. Given your track record the last few days, I find that very reassuring."

"Sometimes you have to take chances to break a case," Joe said defensively.

"You don't *have* a case," Barnes snapped. "Did it ever occur to you that Tom Kilman was just doing his job?"

"Then why did he run away, and why did he try to fry me?" Joe challenged.

"Maybe you scared him," Barnes countered. "I don't know. What I do know is that it's none of your business anymore. I want you out of here—now."

"Mr. O'Hara hired us," Frank said. "He's the only one who can fire us."

"That may be true," Barnes said curtly. "But right now you're trespassing on my property."

His face softened, and he put a hand on Frank's shoulder. "Look, I'm sorry it has to be this way. I know you mean well. But you boys have had some close calls already. If anything happens to you, it's my neck that's on the line, and that's a risk I'm simply not willing to take. You tell John O'Hara anything you want. I'm not changing my mind. Go home. From now on, Bright Futures is off limits to both of you.''

"I'm afraid he's right," Fenton Hardy informed his sons after dinner that evening. "I talked to John O'Hara, and he agrees with Barnes. Furthermore, I warned you earlier today not to pursue this case. I told you you were only to continue with the security check."

"Come on, Dad," Joe protested. "We're getting close. I can feel it."

"You're lucky you can feel anything after what happened today," his father replied. "You could have been killed, Joe."

Joe flashed a grin. "Yeah—but I wasn't."

"Don't push your luck," Fenton Hardy said in a stern voice. "This isn't a game."

"We know that," Frank spoke up. "But the police aren't even looking for other suspects. They're just trying to find enough evidence to pin the murder on Theresa Almonte."

"Yeah," Joe joined in. "I bet they haven't even questioned Tom Kilman."

"There's nothing to question him about," his father said. "Mike Barnes swears the explosion at the farm was an accident—a computer error. He insists Tom had nothing to do with it."

Joe threw his hands up in frustration. "So now we just quit?"

A hint of a smile appeared on Fenton Hardy's lips. "You can't quit now, Joe—you were fired." Then he looked over at Frank. "I want your word that you'll drop this case."

The telephone rang.

"I'll get it!" Frank volunteered abruptly. He ran out of the living room and grabbed the wall phone in the kitchen. "Hello?"

"I'd like to speak to Frank or Joe Hardy," a woman said.

"Then you dialed the right number," Frank replied.

"Oh, is that you, Frank?" the woman responded. "This is Theresa Almonte. I was wondering if you and Joe could come over to my house. I need to talk to you."

Frank glanced at his watch. It was almost nine o'clock. "Now?"

"Is this a bad time?" she asked.

"No, no," Frank said. "In fact, your timing is perfect. We'll be there in fifteen minutes."

He hung up the phone, went to the living room door, and stuck his head in. "Let's go for a ride, Joe."

"Who was that on the phone?" Fenton Hardy asked.

"A girl," Frank said.

His father smiled. "Does Callie know about this?" Callie Shaw was Frank's steady girlfriend. The smile quickly faded. "One thing before you go, Frank—"

"Right," Frank cut in, holding up his right hand. "You've got my word. We'll drop the case—won't we, Joe?"

"I guess we don't have much of a choice," Joe complained.

"I thought you gave Dad your word that we'd drop the case," Joe said as they got out of the van in front of Theresa Almonte's house.

"I did," Frank said. "But I didn't say when."

The front door of the house opened before they had a chance to knock. "I'm glad you could make it," Theresa Almonte said with a nervous smile. "I hope I didn't interrupt anything."

"Nothing important," Frank replied. Before he or Joe walked inside, he asked where Sykes was.

"O'Hara gave him his walking papers. I guess he thinks that since I'm the murder suspect, there's no one out to kill me."

Frank froze just inside the door to stare at the clean-cut young executive type standing in front of him. He spun around and looked at Joe. Theresa Almonte was locking the door.

"Looks like we really stepped in it this time," Joe whispered in his brother's ear.

Tom Kilman chuckled harshly. "You two gave me quite a scare this morning. Now it's payback time."

Chapter

10

JOE STEPPED BETWEEN his brother and Tom Kilman. "Give it your best shot," he growled at the man in the expensive suit.

Kilman edged back, a startled look on his face. "Take it easy," he said in a wavering voice. "We're on the same side. It was just a joke."

"Nobody's laughing," Frank said coolly, and glanced back at Theresa Almonte. She was standing with her back against the door. "What's going on here?" he asked.

"I'm sorry," she said. "We seem to have gotten off to a bad start. Let's try again. I didn't want you guys to run off when you saw Tom, so I locked the door," she explained. "But I didn't know he was going to pull a stunt like that."

Kilman smiled weakly. "I guess I was a little mad about what happened out at the farm."

"*You* were mad?" Joe exclaimed angrily. "*I'm* the one who should be mad! You tried to kill me!"

"If you're talking about that solar collector that blew up," Kilman replied, "I had nothing to do with it."

Joe snorted. "Yeah, right. It was just an accident."

Kilman shook his head. "I didn't say that—but there's no way I could have done it."

"He's right," Theresa said. "The solar collectors are all run by computer from the central control building. Somebody did some fast, deliberate keyboard work to align the mirrors to cause a feedback overload."

"Slow down a minute," Frank cut in. He looked at Kilman. "What were you doing in the hangar in the first place?"

Theresa Almonte cleared her throat. "I think I can answer that. You see, Tom was trying to help me."

"That's right," Kilman said. "I think somebody's trying to frame Theresa—maybe even kill her. I mean, what happened to the solar plane couldn't just be a coincidence."

"So you thought you might find some clue that would lead you to whoever sabotaged the plane," Frank said.

"I know it was a long shot," Kilman responded,

"since the police had been over it and all. But I didn't know what else to do to help. Theresa and I aren't going together anymore, but—well, I still care about what happens to her."

"So what now?" Frank asked. "Do we all shake hands, say we're sorry about the misunderstanding, and go home?"

"Not exactly," Theresa said slowly. "I thought maybe we could all work together."

Joe scowled. "With him?" he replied, tilting his head toward Kilman. "I don't think so."

Frank put his hand on his brother's arm. "Not so fast. Maybe we can work something out. But first I have a few questions."

"I'll tell you anything I can," Theresa said. "I need your help. I'm desperate."

"When we went to see Ben Watson," Frank began, "he mentioned something about 'problems' with the super solar cell. What was he talking about?"

Theresa Almonte bit her lip pensively. "I didn't realize Watson knew that much. Well, I guess there's no harm in telling you then. The real secret of the super solar cell is a new material that Mike Barnes developed. It's much more efficient than a conventional silicon-based solar cell. But it's also much more expensive."

"Too expensive," Kilman added. "That's why Barnes hired Alec Ward."

"Alec was experimenting with different ways

to produce the material," Almonte continued. "That's what he was working on when he died."

"Were you working on the same thing?" Frank asked.

"No," she replied. There was a trace of bitterness in her voice. "I wasn't given a chance to solve it, but I think I could have handled it. Now I guess we'll never know because since my arrest I'm not allowed anywhere near the office or the farm."

"And now Barnes is stuck with a swell gadget he can't sell because it costs too much," Joe mused.

Frank nodded. "That's right. And how much longer can Bright Futures stay in business if Barnes doesn't find a way to make the cells cheaper?"

"Not much longer," Kilman answered. "His credit's stretched pretty thin, and O'Hara won't put up any more money."

Frank studied Kilman carefully. "Just one more question," he said casually. "If Barnes didn't know you were in the airplane hangar this afternoon, why did he cover for you?"

Kilman shifted uncomfortably. "I don't know," he replied stiffly. "Maybe he wasn't thinking. Maybe I'll go to work tomorrow and find out I've been fired."

Frank smiled. "Well, we'll just have to wait until tomorrow to see, won't we?" He glanced at his brother. "Let's hit the road, Joe."

"Wait a minute," Theresa Almonte spoke up. "Are you going to help us or not?"

Frank turned to her. "I'm not sure what else we can do that we're not already doing. But we'll think about it and let you know."

The drive home in the van was a lot shorter and more circular than Joe recalled from the last time. "Is it my imagination," he said, "or did we just drive around the block?"

"Nothing escapes those eagle eyes of yours," Frank replied. "Now use them to watch Theresa Almonte's house."

"What am I looking for?" Joe asked.

"Tom Kilman. I think he deserves to be followed. What do you say?"

Joe gave his brother a giant grin. "Where do you think he'll go?"

"I don't know," Frank admitted. "But I think something's going down tonight, and I think they were trying to con us into doing something for them. Now they'll have to risk doing it themselves."

"But what'll it be?" Joe wanted to know.

Frank nodded toward the house. "I think we're about to find out—because here he comes."

"He's not alone," Joe observed as he watched Theresa Almonte lock her front door and climb into a car with Kilman.

Frank waited until Kilman's car was almost a block away before he flicked on the headlights and put the van in gear. Tailing somebody at night could be tricky, Frank knew from experience. There were fewer cars on the road, so he had to keep back or else be spotted. But from too far a distance in the dark, the only color he could make out was the warm red glow of taillights. So Frank just tried to keep his eyes locked on the right pair of red dots and hope for the best.

The ones that Frank followed led him to a familiar address. He scanned both sides of the street near the brick apartment building where Alec Ward had lived. "No sign of any police cars," he noted. "That probably means they don't have a guard on the place anymore."

"The forensics guys probably picked Ward's apartment clean a couple of days ago," Joe said. "What could be left?"

"Something that Theresa Almonte and Tom Kilman want," Frank replied. "They didn't stop here to admire the view. They're going in."

"Somebody should call the police," Joe remarked casually.

Frank nodded. "Probably. Do you see a phone anywhere?" he asked innocently.

Joe put his sweater over the car phone and gazed around the inside of the van. "Nope. What do you think we should do?"

"Let's wait until they come back out," Frank suggested. "Maybe they'll know where we can find a phone."

Joe propped his feet up on the dashboard. "Good idea."

But ten minutes later it didn't seem like such a good idea anymore. A muffled scream from the apartment building startled Frank and Joe.

Tom Kilman ran out the front door and jumped in his car. There was a screech of angry tires trying to grab pavement as Kilman's car peeled away from the curb and swerved down the dark street. There was no sign of Theresa Almonte.

Joe had thrown open the van door and hit the ground running. He stiff-armed the front door of the apartment building and bolted up the stairs to the third floor. Frank was only a split second behind him.

The hallway was empty and quiet. Bright yellow plastic bands stretched across the door frame of apartment 3E. Each band bore the same warning in black letters: "Police line. Do not cross."

Frank walked over to take a closer look. "If they got inside, I don't think they used this door," he said.

Joe's eyes were on something else. "The window at the end of the hall is open. Maybe there's a fire escape. Let's check it out."

"Not now, fellas," a gruff voice replied, and Joe felt hard metal press deep into his back.

Chapter

11

"DON'T SHOOT!" Frank shouted urgently. "It's us, Con—Frank and Joe."

Officer Con Riley drew back his arm, pointing the service revolver at the ceiling. There was a visible knot of tension in his jaw that the boys saw when they turned around.

"What are you boys doing here?" Riley demanded hotly. "Dispatch got a frantic call claiming there was an armed burglar on the premises. I was in the area, and I charged in and almost put a hole in Joe's back."

Joe forced himself to breathe again. "I'm almost happy to see you," he said. "And I'll be even happier once you ease up on the trigger and put that thing back in its holster."

Riley jammed the blue steel barrel back into

the leather holster at his side and snapped the safety strap over it. "You boys have a lot of explaining to do," he said sternly.

"How about this," Joe ventured. "We were just in the neighborhood and thought we'd drop by to see if anybody was home."

Riley shook his head in a slow, deliberate way. "I don't think Chief Collig will buy that."

"Chief Collig wouldn't buy flowers for his own mother if it was against regulations," Joe grumbled. "I don't suppose you could just forget you saw us?"

"Not likely," Riley answered. "Besides, I'd kind of like to know what's going on here myself."

There was a faint creaking noise behind Joe. He whirled and saw a door swing open. A head peeked out. It was a frail, gray-haired lady. "Officer?" she called out in a quavering voice.

"Yes, ma'am," Con Riley responded. "Don't worry—everything's under control."

The old woman's eyes darted between the two Hardy brothers. "Oh, dear," she said fretfully. "These boys aren't the ones I saw."

"Were you the one who called the police, ma'am?" Riley asked.

She gave a short, shaky nod. "Yes, I called the moment I saw some man and a woman lurking in the hall. When I came out of my apartment to get a closer look, the man saw me and almost knocked me over making his way to the stairs. That's when I screamed. I don't know where the woman went.''

Con Riley glanced at Frank. "What do you know about this?''

"Nothing,'' Frank said with a straight face. "Like Joe said, we were just in the neighborhood.''

Riley's intent gaze shifted from Frank to Joe and back again. He closed his eyes and let out a soft groan. "I'm going to lose my badge over this. I just know it.''

His eyes opened and locked on Frank. "Get out of here. You weren't here. I never saw you.'' He looked at the gray-haired lady and smiled reassuringly. "These men are undercover police officers. They're working with me.'' He whipped out a pocket notebook and flipped it open. "Now, if you'll just tell me what happened . . .''

Frank and Joe slipped away quietly and checked out the second and first floors. Since the old lady said she had seen Theresa run away, they weren't really worried that anything had happened to her, only how she'd get home. They'd call her first thing in the morning.

The next day was the first day of spring vacation, and Joe and Frank sat in their robes and debated what their first move should be. Joe was all for leaning on Tom Kilman. Frank reminded him that Kilman was probably at work and Barnes had left orders not to let them on Bright Futures property. So they decided the best thing to do was drive by Theresa Almonte's house to find out what had happened to her.

Before they got out the door, though, the telephone rang and Frank answered it. It was Chet Morton. "I got the job," Chet told him.

"What job?" Frank replied without thinking. Then he remembered the part-time receptionist's job at Solex. "Are you there now?" he asked.

"You bet," Chet said cheerfully. "They're letting me work full-time during spring vacation. This call is being paid for by Solex, Inc. You should see this phone system. It's got more functions than your computer."

Something clicked in Frank's head. "Sounds interesting, Chet. Maybe we'll stop by and check it out."

"Check it out?" Chet echoed in a worried tone. "What do you mean? You're not going to get me in any trouble, are you? I mean, I'd hate to lose my job on the very first day."

"Relax," Frank replied. "You won't be much help to us if you get fired. It was my idea for you to get this job in the first place—remember?"

"Okay," Chet said reluctantly. "Maybe it would be all right late this afternoon—just before I get off."

"We're leaving now," Frank told him. "We'll see you in about forty minutes."

"What if I said no?" Chet asked.

"What if I said we're coming anyway?" Frank countered.

Chet sighed into the phone. "I'd say forty minutes sounds good to me."

"I knew we could count on you," Frank said.

The Hardys didn't have any trouble finding Chet. His large form dwarfed the receptionist's desk in the front lobby of the Solex building.

Chet greeted them with a friendly smile. "Good morning, gentlemen," he said enthusiastically. "Can I help you?"

Frank realized it was an act for the other people moving across the lobby. "Yes," he responded in a businesslike manner. "I'm Mr. Black, and this is my associate, Mr. White."

"We have an eleven o'clock appointment with Mr. Gray," Joe added, getting into the spirit of things. "I guess we're a little early."

"I'll just call his office and see if he's available," Chet said loudly. He picked up the telephone handset and randomly punched some buttons on the console in front of him. He also stuck his thumb on the disconnect switch before the first ring.

"Mr. Gray?" he said to the phantom on the other end of the line. "This is the front desk. There are two gentlemen here to see you." He paused a few seconds. "I see. Yes, I'll tell them." He put the receiver down and looked at Frank and Joe. "He'll be out in a few minutes."

"That's certainly a fancy phone you have there," Frank observed casually.

"Yes," Chet said. "It has a lot of interesting features."

"I'll bet it does," Frank replied, scanning the console intently. "Does it have call-forwarding? Remote-programmable call-forwarding?"

Chet looked surprised. "Why, yes it does." He leaned forward. "How did you know that?" he whispered.

Frank smiled. "It wouldn't be very exciting if it didn't." His eyes moved to the computer terminal next to the phone setup. "Is that linked to a central network?"

Chet nodded. "There's an interoffice electronic mail system. So if Mr. Watson wants to shoot off a memo telling the whole staff not to eat at their desks, he just types it in, hits a button, and it pops up on every computer screen in the company."

"Can you access the system by phone?" Frank asked.

"You bet," Chet answered. "But you have to have a password."

"Of course," Frank said. "Write yours down for me," he murmured in a low voice.

Chet glanced around nervously. Then he hastily scribbled something on a scrap of paper and passed it to Frank.

"I just remembered something," Joe said as his brother stuffed the paper in his pocket. "I left my briefcase in the car."

"What a strange coincidence," Frank replied. "So did I. I guess we'd better go get them."

"I guess so," Joe agreed. He looked over at Chet. "If we're not back in ten minutes, tell Mr. Gray to start without us."

After another forty-minute drive, Frank and Joe were home again, where Frank headed straight for his computer. Ten minutes after that, Frank was in the Solex computer system.

"What are we looking for?" Joe asked as he watched over Frank's shoulder.

"I'm pretty sure the telephone system is linked to the computer," Frank explained. "A lot of companies like to keep close track of their phone usage. So every call in or out is automatically logged in the computer."

His fingers rapidly tapped the keyboard. "I just have to find the right files."

"The right files for what?" Joe responded.

"Hold on," Frank said. "I think I've got it." He tapped a few more keys, and three columns of numbers filled the screen.

Joe peered at them. One column looked like a list of telephone numbers, and the other two were dates and twenty-four–hour clock time. Suddenly he understood. "Ben Watson's telephone calls, right?"

Frank nodded. "His whole alibi hangs on his claim that he was in his office talking on the phone a few minutes after the time of Ward's death. But with remote call-forwarding—"

"He could have been anywhere," Joe said excitedly. "All he had to do was route his calls through his office phone to a phone someplace else."

Frank touched the screen with his finger. "Two outgoing calls were made from Watson's office that night between eleven twenty-five and eleven-forty—both to the same number." He did some more typing. The numbers on the screen were replaced by the words *Enter telephone number.*

"What's that?" Joe asked.

"Reverse telephone directory," Frank said as he typed. "You give it a phone number and it gives you a name and address to go with it."

The computer displayed a message that said it was *Working.* It hummed and whirred for a while, and then informed them that the number was *Not listed.*

"Terrific," Joe muttered. "An unlisted phone number."

Frank was quiet for a minute before he abruptly got up. "Let's go for a ride," he said. "I need to think."

Frank pulled over to the curb after they'd been riding for a while and punched in Callie

Shaw's phone number on their cellular phone. There was static on the line, so Frank jumped out of the van to use a pay phone. "I just want to make a quick call to tell Callie goodbye again. She's leaving today for a family vacation."

Joe watched as Frank walked up to the pay phone, and was surprised when his brother never even lifted the receiver off the hook. He just stood there studying the phone for a few seconds before he climbed back in the van.

"Do you need some change?" Joe asked.

Frank smiled. "No, I got everything I need," he said. "We have a few more stops to make before we can break for lunch."

"What about Callie?" Joe asked.

"I just remembered she's gone already."

Joe looked at him. "Want to tell me what's going on?"

"Not yet—but soon," Frank answered, pulling up at another phone booth.

A half hour later Frank climbed back into the van for the last time, after checking out a phone booth near Ward's apartment house. "Now I'll tell you, Joe," he began with a huge smile on his face.

"There must be hundreds of pay phones in Bayport," he said. "And all of them have unlisted numbers. The numbers are available, though, because they're printed right on each phone."

Joe's eyes widened. He had a pretty good idea what was coming next.

"And the number printed on that last pay phone," Frank continued, "is an exact match with the number that was called from Watson's office."

Chapter

12

"THIS IS AN interesting piece of evidence," Chief Collig said, pushing the computer printout back across his desk toward Frank. "Too bad we can't use it."

"I knew it was a mistake to come here," Joe said bitterly. "I just knew it. Come on, Frank, we're wasting our time. They're not going to listen to us until we come in with a signed confession from the murderer."

"It wasn't a waste of time," the police chief responded.

Joe snorted. "Yeah, right. We bring you evidence that Ben Watson was only a block away from Ward's apartment a few minutes after the murder, and you don't even want to look at it."

Chief Collig sighed heavily. "It doesn't matter

how much I want it. I can't use it—not legally, anyway."

"I think I understand," Frank said. "It's because we got the information out of the Solex computer system, isn't it?"

Collig nodded. "What you did was no different from breaking and entering. You can't just go around snooping inside other people's computers. *We* can't even do that without a warrant."

"So how long will it take you to get a warrant?" Frank asked.

The police chief frowned. "Since Solex isn't in Bayport, it's out of my jurisdiction. It'll take a while to cut through all the red tape. Tomorrow at the earliest, probably the day after."

"What do we do in the meantime?" Joe wanted to know.

Chief Collig looked at him. "You don't do anything. You're off this case. We'll take it from here."

Joe took out his frustration on the van door, yanking it open and slamming it shut after he got in. "So now we just sit on our hands for two days? As I said before, we're going to need a signed confession to put Watson away."

That gave Frank an idea. "I don't think there's much chance of getting that, but what about a *recorded* confession?"

"What do you mean?" Joe asked.

Frank smiled. "Get the microcassette recorder out of the back. We're going to make a special, one-time offer to Mr. Ben Watson."

For the second time that day, Joe found himself sitting across a desk from a man who was somewhat less than thrilled to see the Hardy brothers.

"I don't know how you got past the receptionist," Watson said irritably. "He's bigger than both of you put together. Then you tell my secretary you have something that belongs to me, and it's a matter of life and death. You've got ten seconds to explain before I call security."

"Only ten?" Joe responded. "Last time you gave us thirty."

Watson glowered at him. "I learn from my mistakes—and you just wasted five seconds." He reached for the telephone.

"We *do* have something that belongs to you," Frank told him. "And it *is* a matter of life and death—your life and Alec Ward's death." He tossed the computer printout on the desk.

Watson's hand hesitated over the phone. "What is this?"

"Just what it looks like," Frank answered. "A list of the phone calls from your office on the night Alec Ward was killed. You told the police you received two calls in your office around the time of the murder. They never bothered to check the calls you made. If they had,

107

they would have found these two calls were made to a phone booth near Ward's apartment.''

"How did you get this?" Watson demanded. "You must have stolen it. It'll never hold up in court.''

"Can you afford to take that chance?" Frank replied.

Watson stood up forcefully, gripping the edge of the desk with both hands. "Are you trying to blackmail me?" he said through clenched teeth.

Frank forced himself to stay calm—or at least look that way. "We're just offering to return something we stumbled across—for a modest finder's fee.''

Watson shook his head slowly. "No. I think I'll eliminate the middleman and go straight to the police myself. I should have told them the truth in the first place.''

Joe couldn't believe his ears. He just hoped the tape recorder in his pocket was getting it all. "So you admit that you killed Ward?" he prodded.

Watson slumped back down into his chair. "I was at his apartment that night, but I didn't kill him. He was already dead when I got there.''

"Why did you go to his apartment?" Frank asked.

"He had contacted me a few days before," Watson explained. "He wanted to sell me information on the super solar cell, and I wanted to buy. I didn't hear from him again until that night when he called and told me to be at his apartment at eleven-thirty with twenty thousand in cash."

"If you didn't kill him," Joe said, "why didn't you call the police when you found the body?"

"I just panicked," Watson replied simply.

"So you went to the pay phone," Frank ventured, "dialed your office, and reset the phone system to forward your incoming office calls to the pay phone number. Then you phoned a couple of people and told them to call you back at the office. That way it would seem you were in your office at the time of the murder."

Watson nodded wearily. "I knew it wouldn't hold up if anybody ever looked closely. I just hoped the police would find the killer quickly and nobody would ever have a reason to question my alibi."

"I think they're going to have some questions about your story, too," Joe remarked. "How do we know you didn't get the information from Ward and then kill him so you wouldn't have to fork over the money?"

Watson chuckled softly. It was a cold, bitter sound. "Twenty thousand dollars is nickels and dimes. I would have paid him twice as much—and smiled happily about it."

He looked at the two brothers. "I don't know why I'm telling you this. I'm just going to have to repeat it all for the police." He reached for the phone on his desk. "I think it's time for you to leave. But before you go—do you happen to know the number for the Bayport police department? Or should I just dial 911?''

Frank tried to make some calls from the car phone, but it was still acting up, so he had to stop at a pay phone instead. One of the calls was to his father.

"What did Dad say?" Joe asked when Frank got back in the van.

"What do you think he said?" Frank responded.

"Oh, probably something like, 'What were you thinking, to pull a crazy stunt like that?' Or maybe, 'We'd better have a long talk when you get home.' Possibly both. Am I close?''

Frank burst out laughing at Joe's parody of their father's voice. "Close enough. He also said he'd drop by police headquarters to find out if Watson really did come clean about what happened that night.''

"We still don't know what really happened," Joe reminded him. "All we know is that Watson was at the scene near the time of the murder." He patted the front pocket of his jeans. "And we have it all on tape if he changes his mind about telling the police.''

"Right," Frank said.

"Who else did you call?" Joe asked. "Theresa?''

Frank nodded. "Other than sore feet from a

long walk home last night, she said she's fine.
She also said it was Kilman's idea to go to
Ward's apartment. Kilman coaxed her into crawl-
ing out on the fire escape to see if there was
another way in while he waited in the hallway.
She discovered that there wasn't and was about
to crawl back inside when the old lady
screamed.''

"Do you believe her?" Joe asked. "About its
being Kilman's idea, I mean."

"At this point," Frank said, "I don't know
what to believe."

The boys decided to pay an unannounced visit
to Theresa to see if she knew more than she was
telling. There were no surprise guests waiting for
them this time. She seemed relieved when Frank
told her she wasn't the only suspect anymore.
But there was something missing in her reaction
when he told her who the new suspect was.

"Don't you want to know why Ben Watson
was at Ward's apartment that night?" he asked
her.

She squirmed a little and stared down at the
floor. "I already have a pretty good idea." She
lifted her eyes. "Alec didn't talk much, but
when he did, it was usually to complain that his
talents weren't appreciated and he wasn't getting
paid enough. I figure he had a deal going with
Watson to sell him information. Maybe Watson
didn't want to pay anymore . . . then, right after

he was killed, Ben Watson came by to see me with a job offer. It was for a lot more money than I was making at Bright Futures.''

"If you suspected Watson," Joe responded, "why didn't you tell the police?"

Theresa shrugged. "What good would it have done? He already had an alibi.''

"So," Frank said, "it looks like Watson was telling the truth. But if Ward was going to sell information about the super solar cell, he had to get it out of the office. How did he get it past security?''

"I never really thought about it," Theresa replied. "I guess there are lots of ways.''

"Yes," Frank said in a distant voice, pacing the floor. "But Ward was neat, orderly, methodical. What way would *he* do it?''

"I don't know," Theresa said. "I didn't know Alec all that well. Nobody knew him very well. His best friend was that CD player he listened to all the time.''

Frank stopped pacing. His eyes lit up. "I think I know how Ward smuggled out the information—and if I'm right, whatever he planned to sell may still be in his apartment.''

Chapter

13

JOE LOOKED UP and down the dark alley before he scrambled onto the roof of the van. The boys had waited until their parents were in bed that night before they sneaked out of the house. Joe reached up and grabbed hold of the fire escape. The bottom section of the metal stairs only swung down to the ground when someone stepped on them from above. The rest of the time a heavy weight on one end kept them suspended ten feet above the pavement. It was supposed to prevent people from doing precisely what the Hardys were doing right then.

Joe hauled himself up and then stretched out a hand for his brother. "So far, so good," he whispered when Frank joined him on the landing. "But of course that was the easy part."

Frank patted the coiled nylon rope that hung over his right shoulder. "It would be a lot harder without this," he replied. "This might have been a wasted trip if Theresa hadn't already discovered that you can't reach Ward's apartment from the fire escape."

They crept up to the top level of the fire escape and then climbed the metal rungs of the ladder that went up to the flat roof of the building. They moved silently across the roof to a spot directly over the third-floor window of the dead man's apartment. Frank looked around for something to tie the rope around. The roof was dotted with vent pipes, each poking up about six inches out of the tar and gravel. But the ledge at the edge of the roof was higher than that. The rope would have to angle up from the pipe and then over and down from the ledge, and there was nothing to prevent the rope from slipping off the top of the pipe. There was a brick furnace chimney on the far side, but the rope wasn't long enough to go around the fat chimney and all the way across the roof.

Joe saw the same thing. "Looks like we're going to need more rope," he remarked.

"No," Frank replied. "One of us can still get in." He handed the braided nylon cord to Joe. "You stay up here and hold the line. I'm going down."

Joe knew the drill. He tied the rope to one of the vent pipes and stood in front of it, his right side facing the ledge. He held the line behind his back gripped tightly in both hands and looped once around his left wrist. He planted his feet far apart and nodded to Frank.

Frank tied the line around his chest and lowered himself over the side, using his feet to "walk" down the brick wall. He managed to get his toes on the narrow lip of the windowsill, and he reached for the window with one hand while the other still clung to the rope. It was unlocked—but he couldn't get it open with one hand. Reluctantly, he let go of the line completely and clutched at the window with both hands.

He twisted slightly and lost his footing. He dropped a few feet and jerked to a stop, the rough nylon digging into his chest and back. Frank heard a muffled grunt from above as Joe struggled to keep a grip on the line and pull him back up. When he was level with the window again, Frank gave it another shot. This time the window creaked and slid up a few inches. Another firm shove and it was open far enough for Frank to get in.

Frank wasn't afraid of the dark—but there was something creepy about the gloom inside Ward's apartment. He felt like a grave robber in a dead man's home. He pulled out his pocket flashlight and reminded himself that he was there looking for the information Ward was going to sell, and that that evidence might point to Ward's killer. It took him a second to get his bearings while he moved the beam around the room. He located the stereo and the shelves filled with compact disks. He walked over and scanned the straight, even rows of disks. Just as he suspected, they were in alphabetical order: Bach, Beethoven, Brahms, Chopin. There were hundreds of them, and there wasn't enough time to inspect each one.

Frank was beginning to have serious doubts that his idea was a good one when his flashlight picked up a rainbow glint on a shelf that started with Handel. He played the beam back over the row of disk boxes and caught the colorful shimmer again. It was a clear plastic CD case with no label. The rainbow glow was the refracted light bouncing off the laser-etched surface of the disk inside the case.

Frank pulled out the case and popped it open. The disk looked like any ordinary CD—except, like the box, the disk didn't have a label, either. An unmarked disk in an unmarked case. Frank snapped the box shut and tucked it inside his jacket. He was certain he'd hit the jackpot.

Frank had to wait until the next afternoon to get the piece of equipment he needed. He went to three different stores before he found one that would rent it to him on a trial basis.

The few short minutes it took to hook it up seemed to stretch forever to Joe. Waiting patiently was a skill he had never mastered. "What's taking so long?'' he badgered Frank, hovering over his shoulder.

Frank stoically ignored his brother and calmly plugged the cable into the back of their computer. "The disk drive is ready to go," he said. "Now I have to put the disk in the cartridge." He tapped a hard plastic case about the same size as a CD box.

Joe frowned. "Don't you just slide the disk into the slot in the drive?"

"Laser optical memory disks may look just like audio disks," Frank replied, "but they're designed to stay inside their protective cases all the time, just like magnetic floppy disks. The whole thing goes into the drive unit."

He went to work on the cartridge with a screwdriver. "I just have to take apart this one they gave me with the disk drive, take out the disk, and put in the one we found in Ward's apartment." His hands worked deftly and quickly. "That's it," he announced, snugging down the last screw. "Let's find out what we've got here."

He turned on the computer and pushed the cartridge into the slot in the front of the disk drive. A message flashed on the monitor screen: Disk unreadable. Reformat? (Y/N)

"What now?" Joe asked.

Frank pressed the N key. "We definitely don't want to reformat the disk. That would wipe out any information on it." He pushed a small square button on the disk drive, and the cartridge popped out. "Let's try again," he suggested, shoving it back into the slot.

The same message appeared on the screen.

"It might have been damaged when Ward took it out of the protective case," Frank said. "I wonder if there's some way I can recover any of it."

This time Joe hit the eject button on the drive unit and grabbed the plastic case with the disk inside. "I've got a better idea."

He picked up the screwdriver and took the case apart. Then he walked across the room and put the disk in the compact disk player that was part of the stereo setup.

"Don't do that!" Frank shouted in alarm. "You could destroy important data!"

"I may not be a rocket scientist," Joe replied glibly, "but I understand the basics of a CD player. The only thing that touches the surface of the disk is a thin beam of laser light. So it shouldn't hurt the disk, right?"

He punched the play button, and the stereo speakers pumped out a throbbing bass sound. Then there was a high-pitched shriek, matched by the metal of an electric guitar.

Joe started to tap his foot. Frank rushed over and stabbed the stop button. "I hate that band!" he groaned.

Joe grinned. "You're getting old. The Insane

Unknowns are on the cutting edge. Have you heard their new single?''

Frank grimaced. "Yes. I don't think 'Mental Fatigue' is going to make anybody's list of classic rock tunes. What I want to know is what happened to the disk with the information.''

The phone rang, and Joe answered it.

"Joe?" a voice whispered on the phone. "This is Chet. Something's going down at Solex. There's a whole bunch of reporters in the lobby, and Mr. Watson is going to make some kind of statement in twenty minutes.''

"Maybe he's going to confess," Joe said hopefully.

"I don't think so," Chet responded. "He sent around an interoffice memo saying he was cooperating fully with the police investigation—but this is something else.''

"We'll be there as soon as we can," Joe told him. "But there's no way we'll make it in twenty minutes.''

The Hardys got there just in time to see Mike Barnes's solar car pulling out of the parking lot.

"What was *he* doing here?" Joe asked.

"Let's go in and find out," Frank replied.

There were still a few reporters milling around. Frank and Joe spotted John O'Hara and weaved their way through the small crowd in the lobby to the bearded man.

"I didn't expect to see you here," Frank said.

O'Hara looked uncomfortable, almost embarrassed. "Did you hear the announcement?" he asked.

Joe shook his head. "No. We just got here."

O'Hara took off his rimless glasses and carefully wiped them with a tissue. "I guess you deserve some kind of explanation," he said, looking down at his hands. "I wasn't completely candid with you and your father when I hired you."

Frank eyed him coolly. "In other words, you lied."

"No, no," O'Hara replied in a defensive tone. "I just didn't tell you the whole story."

"Well, you can finish it now," Joe said.

The bearded man put his glasses back on. "You see, we were in the middle of sensitive negotiations. We were looking for a buyer for Bright Futures. Without the exclusive knowledge of how to produce the super solar cell, the company would be almost worthless. I wanted to make sure that information didn't leak out before we closed our deal."

Frank stared at him. "Is that what this press conference was all about? You sold the company to Solex?"

"Technically," O'Hara said, "Mike Barnes sold the company."

"But you pulled the strings," Joe replied.

"As I told you before," O'Hara said, "I have a certain amount of influence."

"Did anybody else at Bright Futures know about this?" Frank asked.

"No," O'Hara said. "We kept a tight lid on it. Mike is on his way back to the office to make the announcement there now."

"Well, well," Joe said. "This party is full of surprises." He jerked his thumb over his shoulder. "Check out the guy heading for the door."

Frank looked past his brother to see another familiar figure in a tailored suit. He spun around and confronted O'Hara. "If nobody else knew about it, what's *he* doing here?" he demanded, pointing toward the door.

O'Hara looked puzzled. "Who are you talking about?"

"The guy in the designer suit," Frank snapped. "Tom Kilman."

Chapter

14

"COME ON," Joe urged. "We can catch Kilman in the parking lot before he gets to his car."

"Wait," Frank said, grabbing his brother's arm. "Let him go."

Joe shook his arm free. "Are you nuts? Every time we turn around, we run into that guy. He's involved in this somehow."

"I know that," Frank replied. "Go get the van and bring it up to the front entrance. Try to see which direction Kilman goes when he leaves the parking lot—but make sure he doesn't see you. I'll be out in a minute."

"Right," Joe said. "But don't take any longer than that. We might lose him." He ran for the door.

Frank made his way quickly to the receptionist's desk. Chet saw him coming and put on his professional greeter's smile. "Save it," Frank said. "Did Watson have any appointments just before or after he made his statement to the press?"

"Sure," Chet answered. "He's a busy man. He has meetings and appointments all the time."

"Was one of them with a clean-cut guy in a pinstripe suit—his name is Kilman?"

Chet's smile faded. "Why do you ask?" he grumbled. "You already know all the answers."

"Tell that to Joe," Frank replied.

The van pulled up just as Frank came out the door. "Did you see where Kilman went?" Frank asked as the van swerved out onto the road.

Joe nodded. "There he is, right up ahead."

"Good," Frank said. "Now let's just sit on his tail and see where he takes us."

Kilman's first stop was a bank in Lewiston. The Hardys waited in their van for him to come out, and a few minutes later Kilman emerged carrying a thick envelope. Then he led them back to Bayport—and another bank. Once again Frank and Joe waited in the van, and once again Kilman emerged carrying a hefty envelope.

Joe glanced over at Frank. "I think we've just stumbled onto the best-dressed bank robber on the East Coast."

"We've stumbled onto something, all right,"

Frank agreed. "But I don't think armed robbery is Kilman's style."

"You're probably right," Joe said. "It would be too hard to find a gun that wouldn't make a bulge in his suit."

Kilman got in his car and drove off, and Joe waited a few seconds before following.

The next stop was an expensive-looking apartment building with a private parking garage. Kilman's car disappeared inside, and the Hardys were stuck outside.

"What now?" Joe wanted to know.

Frank opened the van door. "Now we go see if Mr. Kilman is home."

Inside the lobby Frank ran his finger down the column of buzzers. "Here it is. Apartment 807."

"Well," Joe said, starting at the top and systematically punching every buzzer, "I don't think we're going to get an engraved invitation." He carefully skipped over the one for Kilman's apartment.

The intercom started to chatter in a variety of voices, saying things like "Who is it?" and "What do you want?" Finally, the locked inner door hummed loudly and clicked open.

"Somebody's always expecting someone or something," Joe said with a grin, holding the door and ushering Frank inside.

They got in the elevator and rode up to the eighth floor. They followed the numbers down the hall to the door marked 807. Frank knocked politely but firmly.

"Who's there?" a voice called out.

"What do we tell him?" Joe whispered.

"Frank and Joe Hardy," Frank said loudly, answering both Joe and the man on the other side of the door.

Joe rolled his eyes toward the ceiling. "Why didn't I think of that?" He looked at his brother. "Now he knows it's us!"

"So what?" Frank replied. "We're on the eighth floor. Where's he going to go?"

There was a quiet pause. Then the door opened slowly. Kilman stuck his head out. "What are you doing here?" he asked nervously.

"We followed you here," Frank said. "We followed you to a few other places, too."

Kilman's eyes widened and he tried to slam the door, but Joe lunged forward and shouldered it open.

Kilman staggered backward. "You c-can't do this!" he stammered as the two brothers stepped into the apartment.

"Do what?" Joe responded with a smile. "You opened the door. I thought you were inviting us in."

Frank took a quick look around and saw a pair of bulging suitcases leaning heavily against the wall. "Going someplace?" he remarked casually.

Kilman's hands adjusted his perfectly straight tie and smoothed the invisible wrinkles in his crisply pressed suit coat.

"You don't have to say anything," said Frank. "We can guess most of what's happened. You've been on Watson's payroll for quite a while. He wanted the super solar cell, but he didn't want to buy a whole company to get it. So he bought the personal assistant to the president instead."

"It happens all the time," Kilman said stiffly. "Industrial espionage is part of any high-tech business."

"It's also illegal," Frank responded. "Maybe you didn't get the information Watson needed, but you tried. What do you think Mike Barnes will do when he finds out?"

Kilman started laughing. "I'm perfectly safe all around. Mike won't do anything because he's known about everything since I ran into you two at the solar farm. Once he found out, he offered to match what Watson was paying me if I'd make sure Solex didn't get anything useful before the deal was signed."

"So, you were a double agent," Joe said. "What about Theresa Almonte? Was she working with you?"

Kilman shook his head. "She's a real team player. She might not like Barnes, but she wouldn't betray him. For all I know, she killed Ward because he was going to sell out."

Joe looked at him sharply. "How did *you* know Ward was going to sell out?"

"Because Ben Watson told me," Kilman answered. "I was working for him, remember?"

"Why did Watson need both of you?" Joe asked.

"He's very cautious," Kilman answered.

"Did Ward know about you?" Frank asked.

"No," Kilman said. "There wasn't any reason to tell him. He could have blown my cover if he got cold feet at the last minute."

"Is that what happened?" Frank pressed.

Kilman sighed wearily. "How would I know? Watson was dealing with Ward directly. I wasn't involved."

"Whoever bugged Ward's phone probably knew what he was going to do," Frank said.

"Yes," Kilman agreed, "if he was stupid enough to talk about it on the phone. I didn't think he was, but obviously he did—at least once. Phone taps are way out of my league. I wouldn't even know how to set one up.

"And don't waste your time trying to pin Ward's murder on me," he continued. "I was at a club on the other side of town at the time. I've got half a dozen witnesses."

"If you didn't bug his phone," Joe responded, "who did?"

Kilman shrugged his shoulders. "Your guess is as good as mine."

"And what is your guess?" Frank wanted to know.

Kilman smiled in a cold, calculated way. "What's it worth to you?"

Joe returned the smile with a bone-chilling grin of his own. "It's worth both your arms staying attached to the rest of your body."

Kilman's smile faltered. "I think you're bluffing, but I'll give you this one for free, anyway. Mike Barnes doesn't trust anyone. He also spent a few years working for the Pentagon—tinkering with top-secret spy gizmos. There aren't too many people who know more about electronic surveillance equipment than Mike Barnes."

As much as they both disliked it, the Hardys had nothing on Kilman that they could use to have him arrested. "Barnes won't press charges," Frank said as they got back in the van, "and Watson can't, so there's no case against Kilman for industrial espionage."

"He'll get off scot-free," Joe grumbled. "With all that cash he's obviously just withdrawn, he can go anyplace and set up a new life."

"Don't forget, Joe, he's going to be the same person wherever he goes. Next time he won't be so lucky. What I haven't quite figured out is the phone-tap angle, though," Frank said.

"What's to figure?" Joe responded. "Barnes tapped Ward's phone, found out he was about to cash in, and decided to cash him out instead. He's got to be the killer."

Frank shook his head. "There has to be more to it. Barnes is a shrewd operator. He could have contacted the police and caught Ward selling Watson the information. Then he could have jacked up the price of the company in return for dropping the charges against Watson."

Joe looked confused. "Then you don't think Barnes killed Ward?"

"I didn't say that," Frank replied. "But if he did, Ward must have had something a lot more important to Barnes than the plans for the super solar cell."

Joe looked at his brother. "Like what?"

"We'll know that," Frank said, "when we find what Ward was going to sell to Watson."

"Well, your idea about the laser optical disk didn't pan out," Joe remarked. "Any ideas on where to look next?"

"Maybe I just didn't pick the right disk," Frank said. "There were hundreds of them. I just grabbed the one that stuck out."

Joe chuckled. "Yeah, I never would have pegged him for a fan of the Insane Unknowns."

Frank slapped his forehead. "That's what I missed. Every other disk in that collection was classical. Beethoven, Mozart, Stravinsky, that kind of stuff. Nothing modern. No rock 'n' roll. And there wasn't any label on the disk. That's why it stuck out."

"So what does that tell us?" Joe asked.

Frank smiled. "It tells us that Ward liked his CD collection too much to deface one of his precious disks. So he went out and bought one he couldn't care less about. Then he took off the label and slapped it on the optical memory disk to disguise it. And now I think I know exactly where to find it."

Chapter

15

"LET ME GET this straight," Con Riley said, pushing up the brim of his police cap. "You think Alec Ward had a compact disk of yours in the CD player he was wearing when he was killed."

Joe nodded. "That's right—the Insane Unknowns. I'd like to get it back."

The police officer sighed. "I knew I should have gone home sick as soon as you called and said you were coming down to headquarters."

"It's just a compact disk," Frank said. "If you don't need it for evidence, what's the big deal?"

Riley gave him a long, hard look. Then he pulled out his wallet. "How much do compact disks cost these days? I'll buy you a new one."

"We couldn't ask you to do that," Frank protested.

"Why not?" Riley responded. "You're asking me to release evidence in a murder investigation. What's a few bucks compared to that?"

"You don't understand," Joe told him. "It's not the money. The disk has . . . sentimental value. It was a gift from a girl who means a lot to me."

Riley snorted. "She means so much to you that you loaned the disk to a guy you just met."

Joe threw up his hands. "How was I supposed to know he'd have a fatal run-in with a blunt object before he could return the disk?" He looked into the policeman's eyes. "Give me a break, Con. If she finds out I lost it, the next time you see me I'll be lying on a cold steel slab with a toe tag—right next to Alec Ward."

A faint smile cracked Riley's face. "All right. I'll see what I can do—but I'm not making any promises. I've got to get the okay from the chief first."

Riley left the Hardys standing where he had headed them off—outside the police station. That was fine with Joe. He wasn't overly eager to see Chief Collig's impression of a man eating lemons. A half hour later he began to wonder if Riley might have slipped out the back way and gone home after all.

Finally, after almost an hour, Riley returned carrying a clear plastic bag. The sunlight made swirling rainbows on the round, flat object he held out to Joe.

"You did it!" Joe exclaimed, clutching the bag. He took a quick glimpse at the label. Frank had been right on target. It was the label from the Insane Unknowns disk.

"It wasn't too hard," Riley told them. "When I reminded the chief of all the paperwork and man-hours involved if you filed an official request, he suddenly decided there was no harm in bending the rules just this once. Oh, by the way, I thought I'd tell you—so you don't have to resort to devious means—that was battery acid mixed with the blood on Ward's floor."

Frank put his hand on Riley's shoulder. "Thanks, Con. We owe you one."

Riley looked at him closely. "As a matter of fact, you owe me a lot more than one."

When they got home, Frank carefully removed the disk from the bag and placed it in the cartridge for the optical disk drive. Then he switched on the computer and pushed the cartridge into the drive. He could hear the faint whir of the disk spinning inside the drive.

Nothing happened. The computer screen remained blank.

"Another washout," Joe groaned.

"Chill out," Frank said. He tapped a few keys. "First I have to tell the computer which drive to use. Then I have to find out what's on the disk." His fingers moved across the keyboard again. A long list of file names and dates started to scroll up the screen.

"Bingo," Frank said softly. He picked a file name at random and typed it in. The screen filled with numbers and mathematical symbols. He closed the file and opened another one, with similarly incomprehensible results.

Frank sat back heavily in his chair. "We're going to need an expert to decipher this."

Joe shrugged. "Why not Theresa? It sure beats the alternative."

"What's that?" Frank asked.

"Using your college fund to get a degree in electrical engineering so you can decipher it."

Frank watched intently as a parade of numbers and schematics marched across his computer screen. Theresa Almonte spent only a few seconds scanning each file before moving on to the next one. Her fingers seemed right at home on the keyboard, moving swiftly and surely.

Frank knew it would be easy for her to "accidentally" hit the wrong sequence of keys and wipe out the entire contents of the disk. But he believed she was innocent, and for a little added protection, he had thumbed the write-protect switch before slipping the disk cartridge into the drive unit. She could look at any of the files on the disk, and she could play dumb about ones that might incriminate her, but she couldn't alter the contents of the disk in any way. So far, if she was worried or surprised by anything she saw, she didn't show it.

Joe leaned in from the other side, trying to get a clear view of the screen, drumming his fingers restlessly on the edge of the desk. "So what is all this?" he asked. "Do we have anything here—or is it just Ward's grocery list in binary code?"

Theresa kept tapping keys, and her eyes remained riveted on the images popping up on the screen. "You could buy a lot of groceries with the information here," she replied. "What we have is a fairly complete set of formulas and schemata for the super solar cell, as well as the results of most of Alec's experiments with variations that might have made it cheaper to produce."

"But still nothing that would give Barnes a clear motive for killing Ward," Frank remarked. "Watson knew there were production problems. So—he thought Alec had been hired to solve them. That's not the kind of thing Barnes could expect to keep secret from anybody interested in buying the company."

"There's also nothing here that gives me a motive for killing him," Theresa pointed out.

Frank smiled. "We'll have to take your word for that, but I believe you."

Joe lost count of the number of files that Theresa flashed on the screen, and he had lost interest when all of a sudden her hands froze on the keyboard. Her eyes narrowed, and she leaned in closer to the screen.

"What is it?" he asked, trying to make sense out of the glowing numbers.

"I can't believe it," she whispered. She scrolled through the file slowly, stopping a few times to display other files for cross-reference.

"You can't believe what?" Frank prodded.

She didn't answer. She just kept checking the data on the monitor. Finally she stopped typing and pushed her chair back from the desk. She rubbed her eyes and shook her head slowly. "I can't believe all that work was for nothing."

"I can't believe it, either," Joe said, "because I have absolutely no idea what we're talking about."

Theresa nodded at the computer monitor. "That's a series of calculations that prove the super solar cell is basically unstable. Under certain conditions, it can fail completely."

Frank studied the screen. "What kind of conditions?"

"Rapid changes in atmospheric pressure, for one," she answered.

"Like in a climbing or diving airplane?" Frank ventured.

"Worse than that," she said. "It's possible that an intense, fast-moving weather front with a big high or low pressure zone could wipe out every super solar cell in its path."

"I'd say that's a fairly basic flaw," Joe commented. "Ben Watson isn't going to be happy when he hears this. Ward's dying before he could tell anybody was very convenient for Mike Barnes."

Frank nodded. "Yes, but can we prove that Barnes knew about the flaw? If we can't, then we don't have a very solid case against him."

"Don't forget," Joe added, "Barnes has an alibi. He was in his office at the time of the murder. I've got to get Dad to give this disk to Con. We can't withhold this information from the police."

Theresa Almonte stood up. "I don't know what else I can do," she said glumly. "I can't prove that I didn't kill Alec, and I can't prove that Barnes or anybody else did."

"I did want to ask you one question first, though. What did Alec steal from you that he was taking credit for?" Frank asked.

Theresa looked blank. "I never said that—who said I did?"

Frank exchanged a quick look with his brother before answering, "Barnes."

"Why don't you go home?" Joe said to Theresa. "You look like you could use some rest. We'll call you if we come up with anything."

Frank and Joe walked out with her to watch her get into her car and drive away. Joe was admiring the sleek lines of the little red sports car when an idea struck him. "The car!" he exclaimed, turning to his brother. "Barnes's solar car!"

"What about it?" Frank responded.

"If Barnes *did* know the super cell was unstable," Joe said, "he wouldn't risk driving the solar car around—unless it isn't really solar powered anymore."

The words hit Frank like a jolt. "Then if the solar car is a fake," he said excitedly, "we have proof that Barnes is our man."

Chapter

16

FRANK SCANNED the dark, wooded terrain with a pair of high-powered binoculars. He was stiff from lying on the hard ground. They had found a concealed spot on a hill in the late afternoon and had waited for Barnes to show up. There was a jeep wagon parked on the side of the driveway, but Frank knew Barnes was at the office, and so was the solar car. A phone call and a quick drive past the Bright Futures parking lot had confirmed it.

The supposed solar car finally came into view and rolled into the garage a few minutes before six that evening, and it was just after eleven when the last light in the house winked out.

Frank waited another half hour, just to make sure Barnes was asleep. He tapped his brother on the shoulder. Joe grunted but didn't move. He was sound asleep. Frank nudged him a little harder. "Time to get to work," he whispered.

Joe opened his eyes and sat up, rubbing his stiff neck. "The next time we go camping, let's bring some camping gear." He scratched a welt on his arm. "Or at least some bug spray."

Frank stood up, grabbed Joe's arm, and hauled him to his feet. "Stop complaining," he said. "Where's your pioneer spirit?"

"I must have left it back in the van," Joe grumbled as they slipped down the hill.

Frank stopped at the edge of the wooded area. "I want you to wait here while I check out the garage," he said in a low voice. "We can't go in the door because Barnes has it connected to the central alarm system." Then he darted out onto the wide lawn that surrounded and sloped up one side of the earth-sheltered house. He crawled up the steep incline to the grass- and dirt-covered roof and made his way silently over to the dim hump of the bubble-shaped skylight over the attached garage.

The skylight seemed to grow right out of the ground. Frank had to dig through the sod and scrape away a heavy layer of waterproof tar to uncover the screws that secured the skylight to the hidden roof. Then he opened the screwdriver blade on his Swiss army knife and slowly removed the screws, one by one. When he had the last one out, he waved his hand in the air, soundlessly signaling Joe to join him. Together, they carefully removed the skylight and set it off to one side.

Frank could hear a throbbing, humming sound coming from inside the garage. He flicked on his pocket flashlight and aimed it down into the opening. The flat black solar cells that covered most of the car stared back at him. To get into the garage without making a dent in the roof of the car, he had to grip the edge of the skylight frame and swing down on an angle. His feet thudded onto the cement floor just inches from the side of the car.

Joe followed him down, easily clearing the wide frame of the vehicle, but he almost crashed back into it when his foot snagged something on the floor. Frank's arm shot out to steady his brother.

Frank swept the flashlight beam across the floor and spotted a thick cable snaking along the cement. The cable ran to a large electric generator, which was the source of the humming noise. He shifted the beam back along the cable. The other end disappeared under the car.

The two brothers glanced at each other. "I bet this is the only solar car in the world that can recharge its batteries in the dark at night," Joe whispered.

Frank didn't get a chance to respond. Suddenly a door burst open, and the garage was flooded with light. Mike Barnes was standing in the doorway with a pump-action shotgun leveled at the Hardys. "Breaking into a man's home late at night is a great way to get yourselves killed," he said in a grim, cold voice. A thin smile curled the corners of his mouth. "Lucky I recognized you before I ruined the front end of my car."

"You should have gotten your bodyguard to come and check out the garage. Then you wouldn't have our blood on your hands," Frank told him.

Barnes gave him a strange look. Then there was a spark of comprehension in his eyes. "Oh, you mean the bodyguard that John O'Hara hired. I'm happy to say that I lost his services when I sold my company. There's no threat to my life now that I no longer own the secret of the super solar cell."

He raised the barrel of the gun, but he kept his finger wrapped around the trigger. "And I see that you boys have discovered my other, somewhat embarrassing secret. A few days ago it could have put a serious crimp in my early retirement plans. Now it doesn't matter. I finished up the last of my business at the office today. The car is all I have left of Bright Futures. But I've got all the money I need, and the super solar cell is Ben Watson's problem."

"And Alec Ward is dead," Joe shot back.

"That's not my problem, either," Barnes replied. "If you're accusing me of having anything to do with his death, I suggest you take your suspicions to the police instead of lurking around my house in the middle of the night. But they already know I couldn't have done it, since I was in my office when Ward was killed.''

He pushed a button on the wall, and the garage door started to rise, clattering loudly as it opened. He nodded toward the driveway. "There's the way out. Go now, and I won't call the police and have you arrested.''

Frank stood his ground. "You won't call the police," he said. "That's the last thing you want.''

Barnes pointed the shotgun at him. "Don't press your luck.''

"I don't think you'll shoot, either," Frank said coolly. "But just answer one more question, and then we'll leave.''

Barnes sighed impatiently. "What is it?''

"After Ward dropped his little bomb in your lap, did you tell anybody else about the flaw in the super solar cell?''

Barnes glowered at him. "I never said Ward told me about it.''

Frank smiled. "You didn't have to. You just did.'' He and Joe dashed out of the garage and back into the dark woods.

The lights in Barnes's house were still on two hours later when Frank handed the binoculars to Joe and squinted down at the dim glow of his luminous watch dial.

"I still don't get it," Joe said as he twisted the focus control. "Why would Barnes wait until now to get rid of the murder weapon?"

"He didn't think he had to get rid of it right after the murder," Frank explained. "But now he knows we're on to him. Then he got stuck with that bodyguard O'Hara hired for him. So he couldn't do it then, but now that obstacle is out of the way."

"Right," Joe said. "I guess I understand all that, but you haven't told me *what* Barnes used as a murder weapon."

Frank patted Joe on the back. "Stick around—you'll find out."

Joe did another sweep of the house with the binoculars. "Well, I sure hope we don't have to wait all night." He thought he caught a movement by the front door as it passed his field of vision. He moved the binoculars back over the area. "Looks like we're in business," he told his brother. "Barnes is coming out the front door. He's heading for the jeep."

"Is he carrying anything?" Frank asked.

"Yeah," Joe said. "It looks like a box."

Frank jumped up and yanked Joe to his feet. "Come on. We've got to get back to the van before he gets out of the driveway."

They scrambled down the hill and crashed through the underbrush to where they had pulled the van into the cover of the woods. They tore off the dead branches and brown leaves that Joe had insisted on using as camouflage and jumped in.

Frank had the engine cranked up just as the jeep turned onto the road. He waited until it was almost out of sight before he switched on the van's parking lights to follow. The moon was half full that night, and Frank decided he could see without the headlights.

"You want to tell me what the murder weapon is now?" Joe badgered as they dogged the bobbing taillights.

"I'll give you two hints," Frank said. "Think back to our last conversation with Con, and it's something you use almost every day—but you usually don't pay any attention to it."

"I've got it!" Joe announced. "He killed Ward with a fast food hamburger!"

"Good guess," Frank said. "Wrong, but you get points for originality." He made a sudden left turn without signaling. There weren't any other cars around, and there wasn't any point in flashing his intentions with bright lights. Besides, Barnes hadn't used his turn signal, either.

The jeep's taillights were dwindling in the distance, and Frank realized that Barnes had sped up. He punched the gas pedal and caught up, easing back on the pedal at what he thought was a safe distance. The jeep put on another burst and jumped farther ahead. Frank closed the gap again.

Joe glanced at the speedometer. They were

going the speed limit. "Looks like we've been spotted," he said.

Frank nodded grimly. "And it looks like he's headed for the cliff road."

Joe watched the jeep's taillights disappear around a corner. "At this speed he'll be there in two minutes. If we don't catch him, the murder weapon, whatever it is, will be buried in fifty feet of Atlantic salt water."

Frank plowed straight through the intersection, missing the turn completely.

"What are you doing?" Joe shouted. "He went that way!"

"I know," Frank said as he slammed on the brakes. "And I hope he was paying attention when I didn't follow him." He swung the van around in a tight U-turn and killed the lights. "He should slow down now."

He went around the turn and slammed the gas pedal to the floor. Frank was counting on Barnes's not seeing the black van. "If we're real lucky," Frank said, "he won't notice us until we're right on top of him."

They caught sight of the jeep again just before it hit the winding road that climbed from the bay to the two hundred foot cliff overlooking the Atlantic Ocean. Joe could see that the jeep had a good lead when it started up the cliff road. But the van was gaining fast, and Joe knew his brother could practically run this stretch of road blindfolded, which was a good thing, since they were blasting around the curves in the dark with no lights.

Joe looked out his window and saw the sea shimmering a hundred feet below and dropping farther away every second as the van wound its way up the road cut into the sheer cliff. Up ahead the cliff and the road jutted out to a point high over the ocean. Joe wasn't sure, but it looked like the jeep was slowing down as it neared that point.

Any lingering doubts that he had vanished when he saw the jeep's brake lights wink on. "He's making his move!" Joe yelled. He watched helplessly as the jeep pulled onto the shoulder and stopped. "We'll never make it!"

"Want to bet?" Frank said through clenched teeth as the van fishtailed around the last curve before the point. His eyes were locked on the jeep as he stomped on the gas pedal and shot down the short, final stretch. "Hang on!" he shouted. "It's going to be a bumpy ride!"

Chapter

17

FRANK'S FACE was a mask of total concentration as the van rocketed straight at the jeep.

Joe's fingers dug into the armrest. He didn't care about the jeep—it was the deadly cliff looming beyond it that bothered him. The driver's-side door of the jeep swung open, and Barnes started to get out. The van swerved violently toward the man framed in the open door. "What are you going to do?" Joe yelled frantically. "Kill him?"

"No," Frank replied coolly. "Not unless I scare him to death." He flicked on the headlights, flashed the high beam, and pressed down on the horn.

Barnes's head jerked around and his eyes bulged wide with horror. He threw the box he was holding back into the jeep and dove in after it.

Frank's right foot smashed down hard on the brake pedal. The tires screeched. The van scraped the side of the jeep, and the front bumper nudged the open door before the van skidded to a halt. Frank bolted out of the van and sprinted around to the far side of the jeep as Barnes was scrambling out the passenger door.

Barnes clutched the box desperately and made a mad dash for the cliff. Frank hurled himself through the air to make a flying tackle. He came down short, thudding painfully into the rough gravel. But his outstretched hands grasped an ankle, and Barnes pitched forward. The box flew out of his hands as he twisted and toppled over. It crashed to the ground and split open. Something spilled out and tumbled to the edge of the cliff.

"No!" Frank yelled as he watched it totter on the edge. A fleeting shadow passed over him, and then he saw his brother hit the ground and skid across the loose pebbles, kicking some of them over the cliff edge into the dark, empty air.

Joe dove forward and snatched the boxy shape. It was heavier than it looked, and he didn't have a very good grip. It started to slip through his fingers. He clutched and clawed at it wildly and finally dragged it back from the brink.

Barnes kicked free of Frank's grip, scurried to

his feet and ran at Joe, his eyes ablaze with fierce desperation. Without even thinking, Joe jumped up and raised the bulky object over his head, ready to club the man with it if he had to. Barnes cringed, ducking his head and throwing up his hands to block the blow.

"Smart move," Frank called out. He got up and walked over to the wild-eyed man. "You already know that thing can crush a skull. That's how you killed Ward, isn't it?"

Barnes's eyes frantically darted between the two brothers, but all the fight had gone out of them. His face was red, and he sucked in air with heavy, labored gasps. He was overweight and in no shape to take on either of the Hardy brothers.

Joe lowered his arms and took a good long look at the object in his hands. "This is the murder weapon?" he asked in disbelief. "It looks like a car battery."

Frank nodded. "That's basically what it is—an electric storage battery. There's a whole row of them in a compartment underneath the seats of the solar car." He looked at Barnes. "You told us about them that night when we met you at your house. But I might never have made the connection with the murder if the police hadn't found traces of battery acid in the bloodstained carpet at Ward's apartment.

"A battery generates electricity through a chemical reaction," Frank explained to Joe.

"They use acid to produce the chemical reaction. The acid is mixed with water, and sometimes the water evaporates." He tapped a row of plastic caps on the top of the battery. "So you just pop those off and pour in more."

"And if one of them was jarred loose by the force of a violent blow," Joe ventured, "some of the acid might spill out." He thought about it a little longer. "But why use a battery to kill somebody? It would be awkward, wouldn't it?"

"You bet," Frank agreed. "But I have a feeling that this battery was faulty and Barnes had it out on the car seat next to him. My guess is that he brought it up to Ward's apartment to show it to him.

"I don't really think he had planned to kill Ward. He probably thought he could talk him into accepting some money for his silence after he sold the business. He did get Kilman back on his side, so my guess is he can be pretty persuasive."

Barnes shrugged. "Think what you want. I'm not saying a thing."

"You don't have to," Frank countered. "I'm sure that the police forensics experts can confirm that this was the murder weapon. I just like to fill in the blanks."

"Don't pay any attention to Barnes," Joe said to his brother. "He's just a sore loser. Go ahead. I'm all ears. So you think Ward tried to blackmail him?"

"It makes the best sense. The easiest way for Ward to cash in on his discovery would be to sell his silence to his employer. That way he wouldn't have to worry about doing anything overtly illegal."

"Makes sense to me," Joe said. "But why didn't Barnes just pay him off?"

"Because he *couldn't*," Frank answered. "He was tapped out, broke, and John O'Hara wouldn't lend him any more money."

He looked at Barnes again. "But I have a pretty good idea of what happened after Ward socked you with the bad news. You got nervous and tapped his phone, and he got careless and called Watson from the office."

Barnes didn't respond. He just stood there rigidly.

"Then you panicked," Frank went on. "When Ward left the office, you followed him."

"Hold on," Joe cut in. "What about his alibi? According to Bright Futures' security, Barnes never left the building."

"No security system is perfect," Frank said. "And remember what he told us the first day? He *designed* the security system—so he must have known how to get around it, too."

"Okay," Joe said. "So then what happened?"

"Here's how it probably went down," Frank told him. "Barnes didn't sit down and methodically plot out Ward's murder. He just knew he had to prevent Ward from talking to Watson. Things must have heated up and—"

"—Barnes hit him on the head with the handiest thing—the battery," Joe said.

"I think I know most of the rest," Joe said, turning to Barnes. "You planted the evidence to frame Theresa Almonte and cut the brake line on the van to scare us off. You had good luck when we showed up at the solar farm, and you quickly rigged the solar collector to blow when you saw me running toward it. That gave you a perfect excuse to fire us—one that would even be good enough for John O'Hara. But what about the plane accident?"

"I think that was exactly what it was—an accident," Frank said. "The plane did work most of the time, and Mike couldn't know Theresa was going to take it up without checking with him first. Remember, he had just found out the cells didn't work all the time, and he couldn't warn her without giving himself away."

"I still say you can't prove any of this," Barnes said stiffly.

"We don't have to," Frank retorted. "The murder weapon belonged to you, and we caught you trying to get rid of it."

Barnes scowled. "So what? You're not the police. Where's your warrant?"

Frank smiled. "We don't need a warrant. You threw the battery out on public property, and we picked it up."

"That's right," Joe said. "And after you stand trial for the murder of Alec Ward, you're going to be staring at a pretty stiff fine for littering, too."

"It's too bad the super solar cell didn't work out," Joe said as they were driving home. "We could sure use it." They had handed Barnes and the murder weapon over to the police, and it was time to call it a night.

"Yeah," Frank replied. "I know what you mean. The world could sure use a good source of clean, safe energy."

"That's not what I mean," Joe said. The van started to sputter and cough. Then it rolled to a stop in the middle of the street. Joe looked over at his brother with a sheepish grin. "I mean we could use it right *now*—we're out of gas."

Frank and Joe's next case:

Professional wrestler Sammy "The Kung Fu King" Rand is in trouble up to his triceps. He's a marked man—the victim of a series of suspicious ringside accidents. Frank and Joe decide to go undercover to find out who wants to put Sammy down for the count—for good!

The Hardys will have to make some pretty slick moves and take on some pretty rough customers to pin this case down. When the boys square off against such muscle-masters as Tomahawk, the Constrictor, and Major Disaster, they'd better be ready for the match of their lives . . . in *Choke Hold*, Case #51 in The Hardy Boys Casefiles™.

SUPER HIGH TECH . . .
SUPER HIGH SPEED . . .
SUPER HIGH STAKES!

He's daring, he's resourceful, he's cool under fire.
He's Tom Swift, the brilliant teen inventor racing
toward the cutting edge of high-tech adventure.
But Tom's latest invention—a high-flying, gravity-
defying, superconductive skyboard—has fallen
into the wrong hands. It has landed in the lair
of the Black Dragon.

The Dragon, also known as Xavier Mace, is an
elusive evil genius who means to turn Tom's toy
into a weapon of world conquest! Swift will
have to summon all his skill and cunning to
thwart the madman. But the Black Dragon has
devised a seemingly impenetrable defense system: he appears only as a laser-zapping hologram!

Turn the page for your very special
preview of the first book in an
exciting new series . . .

THE BLACK DRAGON

Don't tell me I look like a geek," tom
Swift warned his friend Rick Cantwell.
But he was grinning as he spoke into the
microphone built into his crash helmet.

Tom knew he looked—well, weird. Besides the helmet that covered his blond
hair, he was wearing heavy pads at his
knees, elbows, and shoulders to protect
his lean form. But weirdest of all were
the heavy straps that bound his feet to
an oversize surfboard, miles from any
beach.

"I wouldn't say geek." Rick Cantwell's
chuckle came clearly through Tom's earphones. "I'd say ner-r-r-r—"

His voice went into a stutter as Tom
twisted a dial on the control panel at his
waist. The surfboard under Tom's feet
started humming loudly, then floated
three feet off the ground.

Rick ran a hand through his sandy

brown hair, finally getting his voice back. "This is— I can't even say. It's like magic!"

"Not magic—electricity," Tom said, laughing. "Let's try it out."

He twisted a dial on the control panel. The humming grew louder, and the board sped up, skimming over the putty brown track on the ground. The track—a specially designed electromagnetic carpet—was just as important as the board. When the carpet powered up, it produced a giant electromagnetic field that "pushed" against the superconductive material in the skyboard, making it float.

"Okay, now," Tom said, turning up the dial. "Let's see how it moves."

The board picked up speed, riding on an invisible wave of magnetism. Tom bent forward a little, like a surfer playing a wave.

"It's like something out of a comic book. Look at that sucker go!" Rick yelled as Tom flashed past. "How fast can you push it?"

Tom shook his head.

"The problem with you, Rick, is you've got a reckless streak," Tom told him. "For you, there's only one setting worth trying— maximum. That's why *I'm* testing this board instead of you. You're a walking definition of the engineering term 'test to destruction.'"

"Yeah, but how fast does it go?" Rick asked.

Tom sighed. "*You'll* have to tell *me*. There's a radar gun—"

"Got it!" Rick said. "I'll just aim as you pass by and—" Rick's voice cut off with a loud gulp. "Um, would you believe seventy-five?"

Tom was crouched on the board now, looking as though he were fighting a strong wind—and he was. Air resistance of more than seventy miles an hour was trying to tug him off the board.

"This is serious," Rick said. "When do I get my turn?"

"Serious?" Tom started to laugh. "It sure is ... so why am I having such a good time?"

"Hey, don't let your dad know." Rick was laughing, too.

"No, we'll just give him the facts and figures," Tom said. "Like how this thing climbs."

Using the left-hand dial to throttle back the speed, Tom turned the right-hand dial. "Yeeaaah!" he yelled as the board went screaming into the sky.

"Tom!" Rick shouted. "Are you okay?"

"Yeah." Tom's voice was a little shaky as he answered. "Make a note for Dad. This thing climbs like a jet plane."

The skyboard was making a lazy circle about a hundred feet in the air. Tom stared down. If he were a little higher, he could probably see Los Angeles. As it was, all of Central Hills was laid out at his feet.

Right below him, half-hidden in the hills, were the four square miles of Swift Enterprises. Tom could see the landing strips for planes and helicopters and the rocket launch site, but the center of his orbit was the testing field.

Tom noticed that the area was filling up with people. The technicians at Swift Enterprises were used to seeing strange things, but an eighteen-year-old on a surfboard with ten stories of thin air under him—that got attention.

Tom quickly brought the skyboard down to the ground, kicked free of the straps, and went over to Rick. "Let's set up the maneuverability test." He bent over the operations console, flicked a switch, and spoke into the microphone. "Robot! Do you hear me?"

"Receiving loud and clear." The robot sat in the center of the oval track, at a console that was a twin to the one Tom used. Around the robot a pattern of hatches was spread on the ground, making it look like a giant checkerboard.

"What are you supposed to be doing?" Rick's broad, good-natured face looked puzzled. "Playing chess?"

"Each square out there is a separate cell with a small but powerful electromagnet." Tom reached over to one side of the board and flicked some switches. "The trapdoors hide different, um, obstacles."

"What kind?" Rick asked.

Tom grinned. "Watch and see."

He hopped back on the skyboard, brought it to humming life, and took off. This time, instead of going around the test track, he swept across it onto the checkerboard. "When I reach you, robot, the test is over."

"Understood." The robot's hands flew across the control console.

Instantly, a hatch on the ground opened, and blasts of compressed air tried to blow Tom off the board. Tom sent the board into a zigzag, avoiding the blasts.

"Some test, Swift," Rick needled Tom over his headphones. "It looks more like a giant fun house."

A hatch directly in front of Tom opened, and a jet of water burst out of a huge squirt gun. Grabbing the control knobs at his waist, Tom sent the board hurtling out of the line of fire.

Hatches were opening up all around the checkerboard, sending a wild assortment of "weapons" at Tom. Bags of flour, squirts of paint, and even a barrage of cream pies went into the air. But Tom wove through the pattern of "fire" without being touched, like a hotdogger on an invisible wave.

"'You're almost there," Rick said excitedly.

Tom brought the board around for a landing behind the control console. The robot swiveled its head, its photocell eyes gleaming. Then its hand shot out to the power-grid controls, twisting a dial.

"Hey! You're not programmed to—"

That was as far as Tom got as the electromagnetic grid below him went crazy. The board bucked under his feet like an animal trying to toss him off.

Then it swooped into the air on a wild course, completely out of control. Tom struggled desperately, using the dials on his waist panel to try to straighten the skyboard.

He'd almost succeeded when a random magnetic blast first jerked the board, then sent it tumbling. Tom's feet were knocked right out of the foot straps.

Then he was falling, with nothing below him but seventy feet of thin air—and the hard, cold ground.

Tom threw out his arms like a skydiver, trying to slow his fall. "Rick—the air bags!" he yelled into his helmet mike.

Big white patches blossomed on the ground as Rick triggered the air bags. Then Tom's whole world turned white as he crashed into a mountain of inflated cushions.

That evening, at the beach, Tom unwrapped two skyboards—one red, one blue. Rick laid out the control panels and helmets and pads.

"You think of everything, Swift," he said, "even racing jackets." He held one up. "But couldn't you come up with something a little more stylish? Like black leather? This is kind of bulky, and it comes down below my hips."

"It's for safety, not fashion," Tom said. "There's a little ring up by the neck piece. If you get into any trouble on the board, yank it."

"And?" Rick said.

"And a dynasail comes out," Tom told him. "It fills with compressed air in about three seconds and is totally maneuverable. Rob put it together, based on some doodles I did."

Rick shook his head. "Let's hope we don't have to test *that*."

A crowd of kids came from the bonfires to marvel at the glowing track. Tom's sister, Sandra, came, too, carrying a plate heaped with hamburgers. "Some supplies for your trip," she said, a grin on her pretty face.

"Mmm, delicious." Rick grabbed another burger and started eating.

"How about you, Tom?" Mandy Coster asked.

"I'll have just one." Tom glanced at Rick. "Got to keep my racing weight down." He grinned as Rick nearly choked.

Pulling a cable he'd run from the van he used as a mobile lab, Tom hooked it up to the superconductor track he had sprayed on the sand. "We'll let it charge up while we get into our gear."

Rick slipped into the padding and jacket but stared at the helmet. "I can understand the mike and earphones, but I wouldn't think you'd need a tinted visor for night flying."

Tom grinned as he pulled on his own equipment. "Try it."

Rick put the helmet on. "I still don't see—" he began, slipping the visor down. "But I do now!"

Tom pulled down his visor—and the darkness around him disappeared. He could see everything clearly, but it looked like the landscape of another planet. The beach and the hills beyond were all tinted red, and the people around him glowed slightly. A brilliant band of color tinged the sky in the west, where the sun had set. The flame of the bonfire was blinding.

"Night vision!" Rick exclaimed.

"Ruby-lensed infrared visors," Tom said. "They actually read heat waves—the warmer the object, the brighter the light."

"Great. Well, I'm ready to go." Rick grabbed a board and headed for the track.

"This spray-on film isn't as strong as the other track," Tom warned. "We'll probably go up only a couple of feet—if we go up at all."

"Just one way to find out," Rick said, clamping his feet into the foot straps.

Tom tested the radio link with Rick and with his sister, who stood at the mobile lab's control board. "Sandra," he said into his mike, "everything ready?"

"Looks good from here," she said. "I'll move in with remote control if anything goes wrong."

"Okay, then." Tom clamped on his own straps. "Let's go for it!"

He and Rick moved the height controls. The boards floated into the air, bringing gasps from the kids. Tom could hear someone yell, "Outrageous!"

"How's it feel?" Tom asked Rick.

"A little wobbly," his friend replied.

"The spray must be a little uneven, so the magnetic field is uneven, too." Tom didn't mind the feeling. He felt as if he were bobbing on water. "Let's try once around the track," he said, "just to get the hang of it."

"Okay," Rick responded. "Then, when we come past Sandra, we'll speed it up."

His hand went to the speed control, and Tom followed. Their movement was more choppy than smooth, but they could handle it. Increasing the speed helped.

As they passed Sandra, Rick really poured it on. He whipped ahead of Tom, who sped up to pull even with him again.

"How about a little race?" Rick asked. Tom couldn't see Rick's face through the visor, but he knew his friend was grinning a challenge at him.

"Okay. But keep it under seventy—hey!"

Rick shot off again, with Tom zooming in pursuit. The slight roughness of the ride made the race more exciting. Instead of floating easily, Tom felt as if he were on the crest of a monster wave of energy, always on the brink of falling. The wind pulled at him as he upped his speed again.

Five feet ahead, Rick bent to cut his air resistance. Tom crouched a little lower, cutting his own wind profile. The clump of spectators passed in a blur.

"Hey, guys . . ." Sandra's voice cut in over their earphones. "We just clocked you doing ninety!"

Tom moved to slow down, but Rick just whooped and sped up. Then they were suddenly swooping up, gaining altitude at an incredible rate. "What the—?" Tom yelled, fighting his controls.

"You're not responding to remote control." Sandra's voice sounded scared.

"Tom—we've left the track!" Rick yelled. They still swept on, controlled by another magnetic field.

"Time to bail out," Tom said, tearing loose from the foot straps. He grabbed the ring on his jacket, pulled, and felt the dynasail fill and expand. He maneuvered it easily down to the beach.

But when he looked for Rick's dynasail, Tom saw him still crouched over his board. "Forget about it," Tom said. "Get off now!"

"I—I can't!" Rick's voice was tight. "My foot strap is stuck."

A tight, cold fist squeezed Tom's stomach as he watched his friend leave the magnetic field and start tumbling to the ground. "Rick!" he yelled.

A black shape came whispering out of

the sky. Through his infrared visor, Tom recognized the shape of an attack helicopter, painted and modified for a stealth mission.

The chopper dropped like a striking hawk for Rick and his board, a net flying out to catch them in midair.

As Tom stared, the dark intruder changed course, heading up and east while it drew his netted friend inside.

Inside the Black Dragon's complex, Tom saw swarms of worker robots turn, form ranks, and march off together. It was as if a single mind controlled them. Tom shivered. A single mind *did* control them—Xavier Mace. The disturbing question was, what did he intend to do with them?

Then, ahead of him and Rob—his seven-foot robot—he saw the small lab building that was their target.

Rob, back on the sensors, reported, "The entire place is surrounded by a high-energy electron field. And there are faint traces of a human presence inside the walls."

"Rick!" Tom said. "Well, the longer we wait, the more time we give the Black Dragon to get something unpleasant ready. Come on, Rob. We're going in."

In a moment, Tom stood outside the lab building, his duffel bag in hand and Rob by his side.

"Nothing's happening," Tom said as they walked toward the door. He pulled a little white disk out of his bag and stuffed it down the data slot. The locking mechanism went crazy, and the door slid half open.

A white-faced Rick Cantwell stood in the center of the room. His fists were clenched, and an ugly bruise stretched from his cheek to the line of his jaw. "I'm ready for you this time—"

His words cut off as he recognized the robot in the doorway. "Rob?" he said, the word mingling disbelief and delight. "Where's—?"

Tom lifted the visor on his helmet.

Rick's shoulders slumped in relief. "About time you came to get me." He started to grin, but it obviously hurt his face. "How'd you get in here without getting burned to a crisp? There's about ninety million volts of electricity outside."

"I don't have to worry about that in this suit," Tom said. "But you will." He reached into his bag of tricks. "We'll just have to—"

The huge screen on the wall flashed to life, revealing the face of the Black Dragon.

"Do I have the pleasure of talking to Tom Swift?" he asked.

"You do," Tom told him. "Though I don't know why it should please you."

"It's always a pleasure to talk to someone who invents an elegant solution to a difficult problem," Xavier Mace said with a smile. "In reverse engineering the samples of your skyboard that I obtained, I came to a lively appreciation of your genius. That's why I'm giving you this warning."

The face on the viewscreen leaned forward a little. "The secret of your superconductor is no longer a secret. Using the new technology, my automated work force is already producing a selection of attack robots."

Mace's smile became wider. "You have one minute to surrender, Tom Swift."

Want more?
Get the whole thrilling story in
Tom Swift #1, *The Black Dragon*.
Available March 15, 1991,
wherever paperback books
are sold.